# BORN BEHIND BARS

Also by Padma Venkatraman

*The Bridge Home*

*A Time to Dance*

*Island's End*

*Climbing the Stairs*

# BORN
# BEHIND
# BARS

Padma Venkatraman

 Nancy Paulsen Books

Nancy Paulsen Books

An imprint of Penguin Random House LLC, New York

Copyright © 2021 by Padma Venkatraman

Library of Congress Cataloging-in-Publication Data
Names: Venkatraman, Padma, author.
Title: Born behind bars / Padma Venkatraman.
Description: New York: Nancy Paulsen Books, [2021] | Summary: In Chennai, India, after spending his whole life in jail with his mother, who is serving time for a crime she did not commit, nine-year-old Kabir is suddenly released and has to figure out how to survive on his own in the outside world.
Identifiers: LCCN 2021017761 | ISBN 9780593112472 (hardcover) | ISBN 9780593112489 (ebook)
Subjects: CYAC: Prisoners' families—Fiction. | Homeless persons—Fiction. | Street children—Fiction. | India—Fiction.
Classification: LCC PZ7.V5578 Bo 2021 | DDC [Fic]—dc23
LC record available at https://lccn.loc.gov/2021017761

Printed in the United States of America
ISBN 9780593112472 (hardcover)
1 3 5 7 9 10 8 6 4 2
ISBN 9780593407646 (international edition)
1 3 5 7 9 10 8 6 4 2
BANG

Design by Eileen Savage
Text set in Carre Noir

*To my chithi, Visalam Naranan,*
*for always believing*
*in the strength of my words,*
*and to my daughter*
*for literally lending me a helping hand*
*when my body was weak*

# 1

## Beyond a Patch of Sky

Beyond the bars, framed by the high, square window, slides a small patch of sky.

For months, it's been as gray as the faded paint flaking off the walls, but today it's blue and gold. Bright as a happy song.

My thoughts, always eager to escape, shoot out and try to picture the whole sky—even the whole huge world.

But my imagination has many missing pieces, like the jigsaw puzzle in the schoolroom. All I've learned here in nine years from my mother and my teachers is not enough to fill the gaps.

Still, it doesn't stop me from imagining we're free, Amma and me, together, exploring the wide-open world that lives beyond the bars.

# 2

---

# Not Family

U p! Up!" our guard yells at us. I call her Mrs. Snake
because she hisses at us every morning. "Lazy donkeys!"
She's the meanest of the guards but also the most elegant,
with her neatly combed hair pinned into a tight knot.

Looking at her crisp khaki uniform and shiny boots always
makes me feel extra scruffy. I wiggle my bare toes. At least I
have slippers. Amma and the other women go barefoot.

My mother's hands reach to cover my ears as the other guards
join in, calling us worse names than donkeys. Doesn't Amma
know I can hear them anyway? Doesn't she remember I've
turned nine today?

I'm no baby, but I don't shove her hands away. I like her
fingertips tickling my ears, even though Amma's skin is as

rough as the concrete floor. Only one thing in this room is soft: Amma's voice, saying, "Looks like the rainy season is over and the sun-god wants to wish you a happy birthday, Kabir."

"Today's your birthday? Best wishes, Kabir." Aunty Cloud gives me a quick smile and returns her gaze to the floor. Aunty Cloud likes looking at the floor as much as I like watching the sky.

"You think Bedi Ma'am will bring me a treat?" I ask.

"Of course," Amma says. "Your teacher is fond of you."

"Almost twice as old as he should be to still be living here," Grandma Knife cuts in. "Too old."

Too old for what? Everyone in this cell is way older than me, and she's by far the oldest. I give Amma a questioning look, but she avoids my eyes.

Grandma Knife stretches her long arms and rolls up her straw mat. "Can't believe you're, what, nine? You still look as small as a six-year-old."

I slip my hand into Amma's, where it feels safe tucked inside her palm.

Grandma Knife is not family. Grandma Knife isn't her real name, either, just what I call her in my head, because it fits with her sharp tongue. Amma forces me to call all the women living in our room aunty or sister or grandma, though we were just packed in together by the guards.

Only Amma and I are family. At least, Amma and I are the only family I've seen with my eyes—the others I've only imagined from stories she's told me on nights when she wasn't too tired.

Everyone in our cell is awake now except Mouse Girl, the newcomer. She manages to sleep through the morning racket—until Grandma Knife's big toe prods her, making her yelp.

Only last night, a guard shoved Mouse Girl into our room. She stood by the door, twitching with fear, until Amma waved her over to us.

"You can squeeze in here." Amma yanked our mat closer to the wall to make space where there wasn't any.

"She didn't say thank you," I whispered.

"Her eyes did," Amma said, but I only saw them fill with tears. "She's just a teenager," Amma said. "So young."

I'm a lot younger, but I always remember to say thank you.

Mouse Girl is quiet, but she appears to be quite sneaky too. She tries pushing past Aunty Cloud to be the first out the door for the bathroom.

"Respect your elders!" Grandma Knife's bony fingers clamp around Mouse Girl's wrists like handcuffs. Mouse Girl stumbles back and steps on Aunty Cloud's feet.

Aunty Cloud doesn't say a thing, just floats by, ghostlike.

As I shuffle forward, Grandma Knife cracks her knuckles. I try to keep from peeking at her fingers, but I can't help sneaking a look. Grandma Knife's hands are strong enough to snap a rat's neck. I've seen her do it.

Amma says we should be thankful for Grandma Knife's incredible fingers, and I know Grandma Knife helps keep us safe, but I can't help fearing she'll someday pounce on me.

# 3

---

# Rivers

"Don't push!" Mrs. Snake hisses as we join the line to use the bathroom.

Mouse Girl tugs on my raggedy T-shirt to hold me back as she elbows her way ahead. My T-shirt rips even more. I glare at her, but she doesn't apologize, and now I'm sure I picked a bad nickname for her. She's a pushy one, not a frightened mouse.

"Never mind," Amma says. "She probably needs to go really bad."

"We all have to go really bad," I mutter.

The stench of the toilets is as strong as a slap in the face, but I try concentrating on the one good thing about the toilet: It's the only place I can actually be completely alone.

After I'm done, I stand at the cracked sink and use my fingers to rub tooth powder on my teeth. Then I join the crowd waiting to fill their plastic bottles and buckets with water to drink and wash with for the day.

As the water trickles out of the rusty tap, I imagine I'm standing near a wide river, like in a poem my teacher read to us about rivers singing.

*Rivers can't sing! They don't have mouths!* Malli had objected. Malli is sort of my friend, although she's only five. Her thoughts don't float out of jail as often as mine.

"Hurry up, you—!" someone barks.

I shrug. I can't make the pale orange stream of water trickle into my bucket any faster. I tune out the grumbling crowd of women behind me and think about how good it would feel to sink both feet, both ankles, both knees, even my entire body all the way up to my shoulders, in a river of cool, clear water.

# 4

---

# A Piece of Candy

Power cut!" Grandma Knife curses as the tiny ventilation fan in our cell stops puttering.

It never cools the room much, but when there's no electricity and it can't even move a tiny bit of air, I feel like a grain of rice boiling in my own sweat.

"I'm going to faint," Mouse Girl says as a stream of sweat trickles down the tip of her pointy nose. "If I don't die of hunger first."

My stomach grumbles loudly, but I say nothing. Complaining won't make our morning meal appear any faster.

Aunty Cloud presses a handful of candies into my palm.

Aunty Cloud's children visit her on Saturdays and bring her sweets—and she always brings some back to share with us.

"Thank you, Aunty."

I offer the candy to Grandma Knife, who displays her uneven teeth. "You know I can't, boy. They'll just make my teeth rot faster."

Amma never takes any candy either.

I know I should offer to share with Mouse Girl because it's the right thing to do. Amma keeps telling me to be good. But I'm angry with Mouse Girl for tearing my shirt and being so whiny.

Once, I asked Amma why she was always lecturing me about being good, and she told me it was because she didn't want me to end up in jail. That made me laugh. "We're already in jail," I reminded her.

"I can't help that you were born in jail, Kabir," she told me. "But once you grow up, you can make sure not to do any bad things that might get you sent back here."

"But, Amma, what's the point of being good if the police

might lock you up anyway? Especially if you're poor, like us?" I'd asked.

"If you're good, God will be happy," Amma said. "God hears and sees everything that happens."

"So God is like a spy? He'll tell the guards if you're not good?"

"No!" Amma said. "God is the greatest being of all!"

"Never mind about God, boy!" Grandma Knife told me. "Be good for your own sake. If you're good and make friends with good people, you'll have a better chance of a good life once you get out of here."

"And if you live a good life," Amma said, "Muslims, like your father, believe you'll go to heaven." Heaven, she had explained, was up above the clouds, a place where people of pretty much every religion agree God lives.

"Or else you'll end up in hell," Grandma Knife added, "which is supposedly hotter than anywhere on Earth."

It's hard to imagine a place that's hotter than our jail cell in summer when the fan cuts off and the smell of sweat and sewage clogs my nostrils worse than usual.

I decide I'd better be good because I don't want to end up in hell. And because I don't want to risk getting sent back here after we leave. And, most of all, because I know it'll make Amma happy.

I'm hungry enough to stuff all the candy into my mouth at once, but I open my hand to Mouse Girl. "Want some?"

She grabs almost everything.

*Greedy piggy,* I want to say but don't. Instead, I pop the remaining candy into my mouth.

Amma beams me a smile sweeter than the candy melting on my tongue. I'm glad I was good, because her smile will stay inside me long after the candy is gone.

# 5

## Flies

Mouse Girl elbows her way ahead of us again as we line up for the first of our two daily meals.

"Don't grumble, Kabir," Amma says. "Poor thing isn't used to being in jail yet." I don't know why my mother continues to make excuses for her—she'd never let *me* get away with such bad behavior.

"Guess what we have today? Stale rice and water that's pretending to be spicy rasam," Grandma Knife says. "What a surprise!"

"Actually, there is a surprise today," I say. "Look. My rice is topped with a dead fly."

"Aiyo! Take my plate," Amma says.

But Grandma Knife interrupts, "No, no, I'll swap. I've been missing meat."

Grandma Knife grabs my plate and shoves hers into my hands. "On second thought, probably too late to change my vegetarian habit." Her long fingers scoop out the fly and flick it away. "Though it might have been a tasty change."

"Thank you, Grandma," I say. She might be a bit scary sometimes, but she's always looking out for us and making us laugh too.

Amma knows I like her to tell us stories while we eat to take our minds off the horrible food. I don't fully understand a lot of what she describes because I've never left here, and I've only seen other places in books or on TV: bazaars where vendors sit behind hills of spices; temples filled with the most beautiful smells. My mood lifts just imagining it all.

"How about Lord Krishna's story today?" I ask. I love hearing about the blue-skinned Hindu god who was born behind bars, like me.

Amma tells how, on the night of Lord Krishna's birth, the guards fell asleep, and the prison doors magically swung open. Quickly, his mother, whose demon brother had imprisoned her and her husband, ripped a piece of her sari and swaddled the baby in it.

His father spirited Krishna away, not stopping until he arrived at a river swollen in flood. As he wondered what to do, the water parted to let him walk through. He left the baby on the doorstep of a home on the other bank and returned to his waiting wife, and the prison doors clanged shut, locking them in once more.

The demon never found the baby, though he searched for years and years. As Krishna grew into a man, so did his strength and his wisdom, and one day he fought the demon and returned to rescue his parents.

I'd like to do that too. Amma always says being born in jail doesn't mean I can't do great things. Someday I will break out of this place, and then I will set my mother free.

It'll be tricky to figure out how, though, because our doors are always locked, our window always barred, our guards always awake.

# 6

## Houses

Being good isn't as important as being rich," Mouse Girl sniffs when we are back in our cell. "If you get rich, you can get away with anything you want. And you can get anything you want too."

"Look where trying to get rich got you!" Grandma Knife says.

Mouse Girl pushes her lips up in a pout. Then she blurts out the question Amma told me I should never, ever ask. "Why're you in jail?"

Amma's eyes widen in shock. Aunty Cloud stares at the floor.

"We. Never. Did. Anything. Bad." Grandma Knife rubs her hands together as if she's itching to slap Mouse Girl. "So shut up, or I'll shut you up. Understand?"

Mouse Girl gets it and hushes her mouth. Now *I'm* wondering what she did wrong, though I know better than to ask. I feel pretty sure that she probably did do something bad. I've always thought Grandma Knife did something wrong too.

As for Aunty Cloud, I bet she's as innocent as Amma.

Before this, Amma was a maid in a house where a rich family lived. A house is a place filled with rooms, and all the rooms belong to just one family. In houses, doors are locked from the inside. In houses, doors don't have bars through which guards can peek in anytime.

Amma grew up in an orphanage and had been getting too old to stay there much longer, so she was happy to get a job that came with a room in the servants' quarters.

Appa worked there too, as a driver. He drove a huge car like the ones on TV. Amma says my appa was the kindest man. And the handsomest, with the darkest black hair and straightest black eyebrows. She says she saw a photograph of Appa's father once, and the three of us look exactly alike.

My parents fell in love, but because his family was Muslim and Amma was Hindu, he figured his family wouldn't be happy about the relationship. So they married secretly, and he planned to tell them afterward, but before he did, before my mother even knew she was having me, a terrible thing happened.

A guest in the big house accused Amma of stealing her diamond necklace, and the police locked Amma away. Amma said the police didn't care if they'd caught the right person after they found out that Amma grew up in an orphanage and was low-caste.

Because she was poor, she couldn't get a lawyer to help her out. She never even got to stand in court and plead that she was not guilty.

"When they stuck me in here, I almost lost hope, Kabir. Then I found out I was having you, and I started hoping again," Amma told me. "You saved my life."

I didn't actually save her life, not like heroes in the movies or anything. She only says that because she believes you sort of die inside if you stop hoping, even if your body keeps on going.

# 7

---

# Songs

The sky is turning as dark as the circles under Grandma Knife's eyes when Mouse Girl starts whining again about the heat.

Aunty Cloud cuts her off. "Why don't you sing, Kabir? It always helps me forget how stuffy this cell is, so I can sleep better."

I close my eyes and start singing a song by my namesake—a saint called Kabir.

Amma says he's one of the few saints both Hindus and Muslims respect.

My teacher, Bedi Ma'am, told me Kabir's songs helped people come together in their hearts. She taught me some of them and told me what the words mean, because they're in a language called Hindi.

"What's that ugly language you're singing in?" Mouse Girl whines. "If you have to sing, can't you sing in Tamil so I can understand?"

I ignore her. People in different states in India speak different languages, and I'm lucky because I know more than one. Here in Chennai we speak Tamil, but my parents grew up in a nearby state where they spoke Kannada. Amma taught me how to speak that when I was a baby.

I love talking to Amma in Kannada. I love that no one else here understands it. I love how, when we speak it to each other, it feels almost as if we're alone, sharing secrets.

My singing lulls Aunty Cloud, Grandma Knife, and even Mouse Girl to sleep.

I wish it would help Amma fall asleep, too, but in the moonlight I can see her moving her lips in prayer, and I can hear her begging God to keep Appa safe and to please, please return him to us.

# 8

——

# Visitors

I guess my father must be a good man, because Amma loves him so much. And she's usually right about people—smart enough to trust the right prisoners and stay clear of the mean guards.

I know Appa cared about us, because Amma told me so. "He used to write letters. And visit us when you were a baby. He even put money in my jail bank account. By then he'd moved back to his hometown, Bengaluru, because he didn't want to keep working with the family after they decided I was a thief."

Amma saved the letters Appa sent her from Bengaluru. One of them has a picture he drew of the mosque where he worshipped. His letters didn't have a return address because he was living with his parents—and he hadn't yet told them he had a wife. Amma says he was scared their different religions would be a big problem; Hindus and Muslims don't often marry each other.

"Bad enough I was Hindu—but a Hindu daughter-in-law who was in jail? They'd never have accepted that," Amma says.

The last time Amma heard from Appa, he wrote from a place called Dubai, where he'd moved for a new job. He said it would pay enough money for him to afford a good lawyer and get Amma out of jail. And then he'd come back and we'd all live together.

At first, I thought Dubai was so far away he couldn't send letters from there. After all, my teacher said it's in a whole other country. When I grew older and realized you could send letters all over the world, I used to pester Amma, asking, "Why d'you think Appa doesn't write anymore?"

"I'm sure he has a good reason," she'd reply patiently every time I asked. But as I grew older, I noticed how her voice would quiver and she'd turn away, so I stopped asking.

Why did my father disappear? Now I only ask that question in my head.

I like to think he's working so hard that he can't write. He's too busy making lots of money. Because money does help—like Mouse Girl says. If you have enough money, you can pay bail to stay out of jail. If you have no money, they put you in jail and everyone forgets about you.

Aunty Cloud is the only one in our cell whose family visits.

The only visitors the rest of us get are insects. Cockroaches who sometimes land on us in the middle of the night. Spiders who spin webs, wispy as clouds, which I think are pretty, though the grown-ups disagree.

And we also get ants, searching for a bite to eat or a toe to bite. They come crawling in like the sad thoughts that sneak in when I wonder why Appa disappeared. One of my saddest thoughts is maybe Appa stopped writing because he stopped caring about Amma.

But whenever that worry enters, I drive it away as fast as I can, just as you have to chase away an ant as soon as you spot it. If you don't, they invite others to join them. And soon you have an endless line of sad thoughts chewing at your heart.

# 9

---

# Morning Sounds

Our schoolroom is quieter and nicer than anywhere else in jail.

To get to it, I'm allowed to walk across the grounds from the building where our cells are. It makes me happy to have a few minutes free to see how clouds can stretch across the whole sky, how they live in a world without any walls, and how there's nothing to stop them from floating as high as they want, up above the tall watchtowers.

But on Monday morning, while my friend Malli and I are crossing the dirt yard to our schoolroom, we hear the worst sound ever. Worse than angry, barking police dogs. Grandma Knife told me the sound means someone is being punished.

"Hurry up, or we'll be late." I try to move Malli along quickly, hoping to distract her from the noise, but it's no use. There's no way to stop the scary moans from reaching her ears.

"Is someone getting hurt?" she demands. "I heard that yesterday too, did you?"

"Yes. I think it's because we have that strict new warden in charge now. Let's get inside quick."

"Race you!" Malli challenges.

I usually don't like racing because my legs aren't as fast as Malli's, even though she's practically half my age. It isn't fair that she's nearly my height too. But I'm glad to leave the punishment block far behind us, and it's nice to see Malli smiling as she reaches the schoolroom ahead of me.

Malli's always liked school. She's too young to remember Mean Teacher.

I hated school back when Mean Teacher ruled over us. Her favorite student was a bully like her, a girl called Suba, whom I called Tong Fingers. Suba used to pinch me every chance she got—and of course, Mean Teacher didn't care.

"I don't want to go to school," I'd cry to Amma back when Suba ruled the schoolyard, but Amma forced me to go.

She'd say, "You have to go, because you have to learn to deal with cruel people like Suba and your teacher."

"Listen to your mother, boy!" Grandma Knife would agree. "When you leave, you'll need to be smart in other ways, not just book learning. One of the most important things you need to learn is whom to trust."

Then Suba disappeared one day, and soon after, so did the horrible teacher.

Before Suba left, she said she was going to the outside world with her mother because she was too old to be in jail.

Maybe, maybe—at last—Amma and I can leave? Maybe this is what Grandma Knife meant? Maybe Bedi Ma'am will tell me?

# 10

---

# The Scent of Jasmine

Hope you had a happy birthday yesterday," Bedi Ma'am greets me, a smile dimpling her cheeks. Everything about Bedi Ma'am is beautiful and round—curved eyebrows, wavy hair, plump body.

"Here's a little gift for you, Kabir." Bedi Ma'am hands me a string of jasmine. She knows I love how it smells.

"Thank you, ma'am." I stroke the white petals.

The first time I remember smelling anything so wonderful was when I met Bedi Ma'am. I didn't realize the sweet perfume came from the star-shaped flowers tucked into her braid. I closed my eyes and sniffed and sniffed, taking in as much air as I could. When she realized what I was doing, she took off the string of flowers and gave each of us a jasmine blossom.

"Your name means this flower," Bedi Ma'am had told Malli, whose eyes got wider than ever.

"Except you don't smell as good as a flower. In fact, you stink," Shyam, the new class bully, told her, and his friend Srikant snickered.

Bedi Ma'am made them apologize at once. Then she helped us put up our artwork, making our schoolroom's walls as bright as butterfly wings.

From then on, I loved coming to the schoolroom.

These days, there are six of us kids—Shyam and Srikant, who are a little older than Malli and never stop wrestling each other; a three-year-old boy named Chandar, who's always chewing on things; and a baby who doesn't take up much space, except for her voice when she's crying, which can fill our whole room pretty fast. Plus Malli and me.

Bedi Ma'am tries to pull apart the fighting boys as I bury my nose in the jasmine flowers.

"Let's work on your puzzle," Malli says. She means my favorite puzzle, with the picture of a river on it. It's not mine, of course.

Although some of the pieces are missing, I love putting the puzzle together and slowly seeing a whole world appear—a big, swirly river surrounded by trees and flowers. A world so different from our square rooms, with iron bars on every window, and lines of barbed wire that pierce our sky.

# 11

---

# Unhappy Birthday

Bedi Ma'am brought us sweets, like I'd hoped, to celebrate my birthday.

Malli and the other children eat their sweets quickly, and Bedi Ma'am sends them off to play.

"Now, time for your extra-special birthday treat," she says. She unwraps a golden-yellow laddu and I inhale the scent of cardamom and cloves. They're the spices that, Bedi Ma'am says, make my favorite sweet so tasty. I take a small bite.

"You nibble like a mouse," Bedi Ma'am says. Her fingers tap a nervous beat on the table. "Remember the rhyme about mice I taught you when you were little?"

"Yes, Bedi Ma'am. I lock everything you taught me safe inside my head."

My eyes are closed, savoring each bite of sugary gold. When she speaks again, her voice is all fast, spilling words.

"Kabir, I'm sorry. I never thought . . . I'm not sure how to say this . . . but the new warden says that you're going to have to leave because you're too old to stay here. No one insisted on it before because you're so small for your age—"

"What?" I open my eyes to try to see what she's trying to say.

"I hope I've prepared you well enough. You're good with money. You know right from wrong. You're a smart boy. But the world has so many bad people, and I never thought you'd be leaving so suddenly."

Leaving?

"When you're outside, just remember, you must look after yourself. Study hard. Get ahead."

Wait. Is she saying we are going to leave? Going to see—to live—in the world? The world! Me and Amma, at last!

I jump up, leaving my half-finished treat on the table. I feel my smile stretching, stretching so wide it could wrap itself around the whole wide world. "When, Bedi Ma'am? When are Amma and I leaving?"

"Slow down, Kabir. Not you and your mother. Just you. You alone."

"What?" I feel my smile shrinking.

"Your mother has to stay, Kabir. She—well—they won't release her."

"Then I'm not going."

"It's not your choice, Kabir. Not mine either. The rules say you can't stay here at your age." Bedi Ma'am's voice gets harsher than usual. "Unfortunately, you and I can't change rules." Then her voice softens again. "But you've always wanted to explore the outside, no? You're a big boy now. You need to go to a bigger school. And they're trying to find your relatives. Don't you want to meet them?"

Not without Amma. I collapse into my chair.

"When?" I whisper at last.

"By the end of the week. I'm just sorry I had to spring it on you so suddenly. I never knew this rule until the new warden took charge. I begged her to give you a little more time to adjust." Bedi Ma'am's words rush out. "The old warden didn't care so much about rules. This one does. I just wish she'd care about people too." Bedi Ma'am shakes her head. "Anyway, don't worry, Kabir. I know you. You'll be fine."

If she's so sure I'll be fine, why have Bedi Ma'am's eyes become rivers?

I pick up the rest of the laddu and stuff it into my mouth, but it doesn't taste sweet anymore.

"Want to hold your butterfly?" Bedi Ma'am takes down a tiny box from the highest shelf. Inside is a dead butterfly—one that fluttered over the barbed wire and into our classroom a year ago.

Bedi Ma'am had to hold the boys and Malli back so they wouldn't hurt it. But I stood very still, it landed on my finger, and I took it outside and put it on a branch of the tree in the schoolyard.

Bedi Ma'am showed us pictures of plump worms called caterpillars and said that's how butterflies begin. Then caterpillars go to sleep inside a thing called a cocoon they make to protect themselves. And one day, they burst out of the cocoon, carrying rainbows on their wings.

Next morning, I found the butterfly dead in a corner of the yard.

"Last thing it did was visit us," Bedi Ma'am said. "Maybe to show you how colorful the world can be. And how beautiful."

We decided to save it, and I carefully picked it up again and helped Bedi Ma'am put it in a box lined with cotton.

"Kabir," she asks me now, "remember what I told you about caterpillars bursting out of cocoons, all rainbow colored?"

"Yes, ma'am." I stroke the butterfly's wings with the tip of a finger.

"Butterflies look so delicate, but they're strong. And brave. And smart. No one teaches them how to use their new wings. But they're ready to try, all on their own."

# 12

---

# Promise

Back in the cell, Amma's puffy face and red-rimmed eyes show me that someone has told her the shocking news. But I tell her again anyway. "I have to leave. The new warden says it's the rule."

"About time," Grandma Knife growls. "You can't live with us all your life."

"That's right," Amma says, and her mouth turns up in a tight rubber-band smile that snaps back too fast. "I'm so happy for you, Kabir. You'll get to see the world, like you've always wanted."

"I'm not leaving without you," I say.

"No," Amma says. "Of course not."

For a minute I think she's planned a daring escape. But then she just says, "I'll be inside you always, Kabir. In your head and in your heart."

Doesn't she know that's not enough?

Aunty Cloud pats my shoulder, but her touch can't comfort me.

"I'll do something bad as soon as they let me out so they'll send me right back here!"

"Boy!" Grandma Knife cackles. "You think if you commit a crime, the police give you a choice where to go? You think they'll send you back into your mother's arms?"

"Kabir, I never want to see you back here," Amma says slowly. "Once you leave, all I want from you is a letter once in a while. I don't even want you visiting and making people wonder if you did something wrong. Promise me you won't ever set foot in jail again after you leave."

My eyes gaze at the dirt-stained hem of her underskirt.

Amma hugs me, but she says, "When you get out, don't waste a minute looking back. Get ahead, that's what you need to do. Make me proud of you."

At night, when I look up at my patch of sky, I see no moon, no stars, not a single point of light. How can I get ahead when I'm forced to leave behind the person I love most?

# 13

------

# Three People

That evening, I fall into a restless sleep but wake to something tickling my toes. A mouse's quivering whiskers. Ugh!

I yank my feet away and wave my hand at it. "Go!" I whisper, trying to shoo it away.

Grandma Knife bolts upright. Her sharp ears hear everything. Her eyes take in the scene. She reaches for the stone she keeps beside her when she sleeps. Usually, I shut my eyes and listen for the pitiful squeak, because Grandma Knife's stone never misses its mark.

Maybe it's the shock and anger of learning I have to leave, but something wakes up inside me, something as powerful as a searchlight, and I jump up and stamp my feet. The mouse darts out of our cell through a hole in the wall.

"What's got into you, boy?" Grandma Knife sounds amused, not annoyed. "We can't risk having rodents running around. Who's going to help us if they bite and we fall ill?"

I shrug. Mice may carry disease, and rats scare me, but today I don't think even they deserve to die.

"You must be so upset, poor boy." Grandma Knife's voice gets sort of wobbly. She comes and sits near me. "But you're going to be okay. Once you leave, you'll need to think quickly, Kabir. Act fast to help yourself, just like you helped that mouse."

"I—I'm scared," I confess.

"Of course you are! You know what? I used to be scared of mice."

"Really?" Is she joking?

"I never thought I'd be so great at getting rid of them," she says softly. "I never thought I'd end up in jail either."

And I never expected to be leaving jail so soon—or without Amma. But maybe now I can find a way to make things better. "I want to find a way to save Amma," I tell Grandma Knife. "You think I can do that?"

"You'll find a way, boy." Grandma Knife bares her teeth at me in a rare—and real—smile. "God gave you a big brain, just like he gave me a big mouth."

I'm not sure what surprises me more: Grandma Knife giving me a compliment or Grandma Knife mentioning God.

I return Grandma Knife's smile. "Maybe I can find Appa. Why d'you suppose he stopped writing? You think he was a good man, like Amma always says?"

"All I know is your mother's a good judge of character—and that's a gift she passed on to you. So if something doesn't feel right, trust yourself and run as fast as that mouse." She hasn't answered my question, but I don't mind, because she gives me another compliment. "You'll be fine, boy. I have faith in you."

I used to count on two people believing in me—Amma and Bedi Ma'am. Now I realize there are three. Grandma Knife believes in me too.

"And remember, Kabir, if you have to chuck a stone at someone to protect yourself, do it."

I picture myself throwing a tiny stone at Mrs. Snake's back.

In my head, she gives a satisfying yelp. "But my aim is not as good as yours, Grandma."

"I guess not." She strokes her chin. "You can run a lot faster than me, though."

# 14

## My Father's Mosque

How much money should I return to you?" Bedi Ma'am asks.

"Five rupees and forty-one paisa." I can do arithmetic in my head, but it's better using real paper rupees and shiny coins. I like the sound of coins clinking together.

"Right." She starts lecturing me. "Never forget to count your change. Bargain, like we've practiced, so if you have to buy anything, you'll pay the lowest possible price. Never gamble. Never trust anyone who says they'll give you a lot of money for an easy job. Save money, don't spend it all . . ."

The baby squawks, but Bedi Ma'am ignores her. She pays more attention to me now than ever before, though she smiles at me a lot less.

"Now, here's what a bus ticket looks like. If you get on a bus, you have to pay a man called the conductor." She shows me a picture of a man in a khaki uniform.

"He looks like a policeman," I say.

"He sort of is a policeman, for the bus. Never do things on a dare—like riding a bus without a ticket. Policemen like locking up poor, low-caste boys, so don't give them any excuses, hear me?"

"I won't." I smooth out the wrinkled ticket. "Ma'am, how long is a bus ride to Bengaluru? Where the Juma Masjid is? Amma says it's the mosque where my grandparents worship."

"Bengaluru is a few hours away by train or bus," she says. "It's in another state, and unfortunately people in our state are fighting with people from there about sharing water."

"Oh, I thought it was only in jail that we didn't have enough water." Often in the summer we go for days without a wash because we don't have enough running water.

"No, water shortages are a big problem in lots of places." Bedi Ma'am pulls out a map to explain further. "We're here in Chennai, this dot is Bengaluru city, and this blue line is a river. The river runs through our state and theirs. The government decides how much water we each get—but the people still fight. A few days ago, a mob here beat up a man just because he spoke Kannada and came from Bengaluru, like your parents. So be careful outside. Make sure to just speak the local language. The streets are full of angry people waiting to hurt someone else."

My teacher makes the outside world sound scary—full of adults who aren't any better at sharing than my classmates Shyam and Srikant, who play tug-of-war with every book and toy.

The next day, Bedi Ma'am brings me a picture of the Juma Masjid mosque. It's beautiful and bright, and more colorful than the faded old drawing Amma saved for years along with Appa's letters. I imagine I'm standing in front of it with my father—but then Bedi Ma'am pulls the photograph gently out of my hands and demands, "Pay attention, Kabir!"

It's a scorching-hot day and the air feels stale because there's been another power cut. A row of ants crawls in from the courtyard, and Shyam and Srikant start stomping on them. Usually Bedi Ma'am would tell them off, but today she ignores them. She doesn't even try rescuing books that Chandar munches on. She's too busy telling me a million things.

Right now, my teacher clearly doesn't care about ants or anything except making sure she can pour as much information into me as possible in the time we have left.

My head feels like an overfull bucket.

# 15

## Uncles and Orphanages

At recess, I try and try to explain to Malli why I have to leave. "One day you'll leave, too, with your mother." I hope that's true.

But Malli isn't listening. All morning she looked away whenever I tried to talk to her, which wasn't often, with Bedi Ma'am so focused on educating me.

Now she marches off and starts playing ball with Chandar, even though he can barely throw and definitely can't catch. For a while, I sit all alone under the skinny neem tree.

Finally I get tired of being ignored. I snatch the ball out of Malli's hands and burst out, "It's not my fault Bedi Ma'am is spending so much time with me! I didn't ask her to!"

"You're going away!"

"Because I have to! Can't you understand? I have no choice. None of us do!"

She pouts. Any other time, I might have laughed because she looks funny with her mouth all puckered up. But I tell her, "I'm scared about leaving. And I'll miss you. I'm as sad as you are!"

"Who says I'm sad?" Malli lashes out. "I'm happy you're leaving. I hate you!"

Her words hurt. But when we return to the classroom, Bedi Ma'am tells me something that drives away every other thought. "They've found your family, Kabir."

"My father?" My heart starts spinning, fast as a top.

"No. Your uncle."

"My— I never even knew I had an uncle."

"I guess you do." Bedi Ma'am smiles. "He isn't a direct uncle—they said he's your father's cousin, not your father's brother—but I'm so glad they found him. I really didn't want you ending up in an orphanage."

An orphanage? Amma grew up in an orphanage and said it was awful. Guess it's a good thing I didn't even know that was a possibility.

# 16

———

# Home

As soon as I return to our cell, I tell Amma the news in our own language because I don't want everyone else knowing.

Mouse Girl scowls. It irritates her that Amma and I can chat in a language she doesn't understand, though Amma's told her we're not saying anything about her.

"Why can't they just send me to Appa?" I ask.

"Your father is somewhere in Dubai, Kabir. That's too far away. But your uncle is right here, in this state, in Chennai city, close to our jail."

"Did Appa ever tell you about his cousin? Did you ever meet him? Is he nice?"

"I never met anyone in his family. I never even knew he had a cousin who lived around here." Amma gives me a sad smile. "They told me he works at the same place your father and I worked."

"I don't want to go *there*. The family didn't trust you."

Amma shrugs. "Rich people never trust poor, low-caste maids like me. They weren't cruel to your father—or even to me, really. They just assumed I stole and didn't bother to find out the truth. It's what rich people do."

"Don't you ever get angry, Amma?"

"I used to. I even fought with our guard at first." Amma smiles at my surprise.

It's hard to believe Amma ever fought with Mrs. Snake—I would love to see that.

But right now, seeing Amma's sad smile makes me feel angry enough for the two of us. I'll never forgive that rich family for locking Amma up without giving her any chance to explain. It's their fault I've been in jail all my life.

"It's nice of this uncle to take you in," Amma says. "If he's your father's cousin, I'm sure he's a good man."

"You think he'll like me? Even though I'm half Hindu?"

"I'm sure he'll love you. How could he not?" Amma closes her eyes and brings her palms together. "I'm grateful to God you'll finally have a proper home."

"This is home," I say.

"No," she says. "This is jail. Home is where you're looked after by people who love you."

"Then this is home," I argue. "Because you love me."

"It's still jail," she repeats. "People will assume you're bad if they find out you were born here, so don't be talking about it."

Suddenly, I'm scared I might cry. And even though we've been speaking in Kannada, Amma and I, everyone else in our cell must see I'm upset.

Aunty Cloud waddles over and puts a warm arm around my shoulders.

Grandma Knife says, "Don't worry, boy. There's nothing you can't handle."

I must look really pitiful, because even Mouse Girl reaches out to give me a swift pat on the back.

# 17

---

# Last Words

"Ma'am, do you think there's a way I can help Amma get out of jail?" I ask my teacher on my last day of jail school.

"Why not?" Bedi Ma'am says. "You can try to do anything. If you study hard, maybe you can become a lawyer when you grow up."

I'm about to let her know that I'm not going to let Amma stay here until I'm all grown up, but Malli edges up to us and pats my back, the way Bedi Ma'am pats the baby's back when she howls. I guess Malli decided she doesn't hate me anymore.

"You can do anything, Kabir," she tells me. "Except beat me in a race."

"You know what?" I grin at her. "I bet you'll beat everyone at everything when you get out of here."

Bedi Ma'am holds out the butterfly box to me.

"You'll grow as quickly as a caterpillar when you leave here," Bedi Ma'am says. "And you'll brighten the world, I'm sure of it."

I open the box. "Goodbye," I whisper to the butterfly. "And thank you."

"You can have it, Kabir. Take it with you."

The butterfly is the first beautiful thing I've ever owned. I turn the box over and over in my hands as I thank her.

"Will I ever see you again?" Malli hugs me tight.

"Why not?" I echo Bedi Ma'am's words, and I hug her back just as hard. Bedi Ma'am joins us, and the three of us are wrapped up together for a bit.

After we let each other go, I touch the butterfly one last time. I can do what I want with it. Because it's all mine.

It means so much to me that I give it to Malli.

Her eyes grow bigger than ever.

For a moment I wonder if Bedi Ma'am is upset that I gave her gift away. But Bedi Ma'am smiles.

She understands what I can't say.

# 18

—

# Behind Me

Our last night together in our cell, Amma draws me onto her lap as if I'm a baby again. I'm glad, because I feel like a baby.

I wish I could scream and cry like the baby in the school-room. Instead, I stare at my sky square, in which a thin slice of moon is glowing.

Amma doesn't tell me any stories. Just sings me a lullaby she'd sing when I was a baby. "Nila, nila va va . . . nillamal odi va." *Moon, moon, come running to me . . . climb over the mountain and bring a jasmine flower.*

The words are confusing—the moon doesn't have hands to bring flowers. I feel so helpless that I can't even understand what a lullaby means.

But I don't want to think about the song or where I'll be going on my own or how far away Amma will soon be. I want the sad, scary questions in my head to shut up so I can listen only to Amma's beautiful voice. I want my silly heart to stop flopping around in my chest so that all I'll feel is the warmth of Amma's arms around me.

I stare at my square of sky until I drift into what feels like the shortest sleep of my life.

Familiar noises wake me to the worst day of my life. Chains rattle, keys clink, locks squeak, hinges complain.

Amma knocks the breath out of me squeezing me to her chest. I don't complain. I want to be held tighter, until she squeezes all the feeling out of me.

"Every single day," Amma says, "I'll think of you out there, and that will make me happy." Her voice is steady as she steers me toward the door, where a policeman waits.

My voice sticks in my throat like the wrong key in a lock. I can't get any words out.

Aunty Cloud pulls me into a quick hug.

Mouse Girl says, "Be careful out there. Stay away from policemen. Be safe."

Grandma Knife puts her hands on my shoulders. Her touch is surprisingly gentle. "Kabir, I'll look after your mother. Your job from now on is to look after yourself." Then she grins, displaying her uneven teeth. "I'd give you my blessings, boy, if I thought they'd do you any good, but all I can do properly is curse."

Amma forces a laugh and gives me a gentle push. "I don't have anything to give you, either, except words, Kabir. So remember all I taught you. Go on. Go ahead. Don't look back."

But I do look back before the door clangs shut. Through tear-blurred eyes I see Amma crumpled on the ground like a scrap of paper.

# 19

## In the Outside

The policeman leads me across a yard where flies swarm over a rubbish heap. We enter a low building where he barks orders at some other policemen. My policeman signs my name, Kabir Khan, in a great big book.

Heavy metal doors open and lock behind us as the policeman leads me through a maze of rooms and out past a tall, spiky gate.

It's all happening too fast. Every step is taking me farther away from Amma. I don't want to leave, but my legs keep walking.

Then we're standing in front of a white police van that's as big as our cell. Its windows are covered with wire mesh that reminds me of pictures of fishnets I've seen in books.

The policeman motions for me to climb into the back of the van. The van's walls and floor shudder and jerk as if it's alive, and to my shock, as it lurches forward, my body slides around. I cling to my seat and try not to get dizzy as the world around us moves.

I tell myself I'm free, I'm outside where I dreamed of going, but I feel like a fish in a net being lifted out of the water I've lived in all my life.

We dart in and out between cars, trucks, and buses, like I've seen on TV. Except they're not flat. Out here, they're bigger than me, growling on the roads like monsters with huge eyes. My stomach churns.

In my head, outside was peaceful. But the real world is busy with movement and noise. The blaring horns hurt my ears, and the fumes from the cars make me feel sick.

The driver of the van pulls up in front of a huge redbrick building with a sign that says POLICE STATION. On woozy legs, I stumble behind the policeman, into the building, and into a stuffy room where fans sway from the ceiling.

My head is pounding so hard I want to lie down. I'm glad when the policeman orders me to sit and leaves me alone in a chair for a while.

"Khan!" the policeman says. I think he means me, but when I look up, I see all eyes are on a man with muscles rippling under his shirt as he strides across the floor. He talks to the policeman for a minute and then stares at me.

This must be my uncle. But why doesn't he return my smile?

Instead, he just issues a command. "Follow me, boy."

Wishing he'd called me nephew or even Kabir, I say, "Yes, Uncle."

People walk by us as we move along the sidewalk—women, children, and more men than I've met my whole life in jail. On the street, it's mostly men, too, driving vehicles of all kinds. My body feels like it's in a dream, like it half belongs to someone else.

My mind is brimful of questions, but I keep them from sloshing out of me because my uncle growls *no* to the first two things I ask: Please, can I meet my father soon? and Uncle, do you have children?

When he takes my hand to help me cross the road, where a motorbike nearly runs into us, his grip feels like I imagine handcuffs feel: cold, hard, unbreakable.

But his grip protected me. If it wasn't for him, I'd have been run over.

Maybe he's like Grandma Knife. Edgy and sharp, but with kindness somewhere inside him, ready to slip out when I need it.

# 20

---

# House

Uncle speaks only when we turn onto a shady avenue lined with trees. "You're not to say a word to anyone about where you came from. If they ask, you say you're my nephew. From the village."

"Of course!" Why wouldn't I say that? I am his nephew!

"Don't forget. You're mine now," my uncle says, grinning in a way that feels all wrong. It feels wrong that he speaks in Tamil too. If he's family, he should know Kannada. Why hasn't he spoken to me in Kannada?

"This is the house where I work," my uncle says. He stops by a walled compound. A guard opens the tall white gate to let us in.

Sunlight glints off the huge glass windows, and bright flowers dot the gardens. So this is the house where my parents met and fell in love. It's even prettier than I imagined. Full of color. Full of living things—unlike the empty grounds I'm used to. It's nicer than my best dreams.

Through an open door at the back of the house, I see a kitchen. The tile floor is so clean it sparkles—the opposite of the jail kitchen, which had a two-fingers-thick layer of grime.

A woman is stirring something on a stove. I can't help staring at her sari—bright as the garden flowers. Amma must have worn colorful saris, too, when she was a maid, instead of the plain uniform of old shirts and long skirts that all the women wear in jail.

The woman turns as if she feels my eyes on her. "We have a visitor!" Her face lights up with a warm smile. "What's your name, young man?"

"Kabir." I smile back.

"My nephew." Uncle gives me a little shove. "Move along, boy."

But the woman comes to the door and asks, "Where're you visiting from, Kabir? Had a long journey?"

I hesitate for a second. I know I'm not supposed to go blabbing about being from jail, so I just say, "Didn't come from very far away, ma'am."

"Please call me Aunty. It's so nice to see a young face! Shall I fix you a snack?"

I glance uneasily at my uncle. "Not now," he says firmly. "We have things to do."

"All right. Come back later, Kabir. You look like you could use some fattening up."

"Thank you, Aunty," I tell her. I wish I could stay, but my uncle steers me down a path that curves behind the great house and leads to a small building.

"Will I work here too, sir?" I ask as I follow him.

"Enough with the questions, boy. Shut up like you did on the way here. They like quiet children where you're going, so hush your mouth."

Something about the way uncle says *where you're going* makes me think he's sending me away, someplace far from here.

And that place doesn't sound nice, like it might be my father's or grandparents' home.

He doesn't say one word about my father. He doesn't act like he even knows my father. But if he doesn't, then why did he take me in at all?

# 21

## Locks

These are the servants' quarters, and this is my room," Uncle says, leading me into a room a little larger than my old cell, with a bed and a great big window and a ceiling fan. But somehow the room feels just as unfriendly. "Well, are you hungry?"

"Yes, Uncle."

"I'll bring you some food. But wash up first." He shows me into a small bathroom where there's a bar of green soap.

I take my time in there, and though I miss Amma already, a part of me can't help but be glad that I don't need to hurry. No one here is yelling at me about wasting water. And the tap water is nice and clear, not brown.

When I'm all clean and back in the room, my uncle brings me rice and yellow lentils. The food is warm and spicy and salted just right, better than anything I've ever tasted, except for Bedi Ma'am's treats.

When I'm done, Uncle says, "I have to go to work now, but you stay here and be quiet. Understand? No talking to anyone. You want to take a nap, pull out the mattress that's under the bed. Don't touch my bed."

"Thank you for the food, Uncle."

"Wouldn't look good if you fainted from hunger."

He locks me in the room, and I can't escape the feeling I've moved into a different kind of prison. One that's miles away from Amma's soft voice.

# 22

---

# Unquiet

It's not easy to nap, though my head is tired from all the noise not just in this outside world, but also inside me, where my heart is yammering with fear and confusion.

I've never been in a room on my own for this long.

*Amma, Amma, Amma,* I whisper, over and over.

I search for her in my heart. I try to listen to her voice in my head.

For the first time, imagining doesn't help. Imagining she's nearby just reminds me she's far away.

I lie down and gaze out the large window, at the rounded

treetops. It's calming to watch the leaves flutter when the breeze tickles them. My eyes feel heavy, and I can't keep them open.

By the time I wake, sunlight is slanting through the trees, making their shadows lean and long.

I forget where I am for a moment, and then Grandma Knife's warning echoes inside my head. This outside world is full of people I mustn't trust. But how can I trust myself to do anything in this strange world, filled with things I've never touched or smelled before?

I hear the familiar sound of a key turning the lock. Uncle enters. "Here," he says, tossing a brand-new shirt and pair of shorts at me. "Put these on after you eat."

"Thank you, Uncle," I say. I pick up the clothes. They don't have an old-new smell. They feel new-new! Did someone tell him it was my birthday recently?

He has brought me more food too—fluffy rice and spicy vegetable curry.

"Thank you, Uncle! Thank you!" Maybe he is kind, after all, my uncle. Just not friendly.

When I've eaten and changed, he says, "Let's go."

Where? I know better than to ask.

We hurry along noisy, dusty streets that get twistier and dirtier as we move along, leaving the house far behind.

# 23

---

# Snake Man

We enter a small, dingy room where a man is lighting a bidi, smoke snaking out of his lips.

"This is the boy," my uncle says.

Snake Man's eyes sweep over me.

"He's quiet and obedient," my uncle says. "He'll be able to put fireworks together or sew buttons or whatever it is you want him to do."

"Yes, sir," I say. "I'm willing to work hard so I can get ahead."

"Good." Snake Man gives me a twisted smile. "Now, you go wait in the kitchen. I need to discuss something with your uncle."

He pulls the flimsy door half shut behind me. I sit on the floor of the grimy kitchen, where I can still hear everything the men say, since they aren't bothering to speak that softly.

"Where'd you get him?" Snake Man asks.

"His father used to work where I work. Police came one day asking for a man called Khan and didn't bother to check when I said I was his father's cousin. I have the same last name and figured that was enough."

What! He's not really my uncle?

Snake Man laughs the way Mrs. Snake did whenever Aunty Cloud stumbled and stubbed her toes.

They begin haggling over a price like I've seen the women in jail do when someone has been able to smuggle in a thing from outside that everyone else wants. What's my fake uncle selling?

The answer strikes me like a whip when the men finally settle on a price.

My "uncle" is selling me.

# 24

---

# Hot Coffee

Bring him to me, day after tomorrow," I hear Snake Man saying.

"Why not take him now?" Fake Uncle grumbles. "It's too risky, me keeping him there!"

"What's risky about having your nephew from the village visit? You want your money, you'll get it when you bring him back—or give him to me now for a quarter of the price."

"All right, all right," Fake Uncle says. He opens the kitchen door. "Let's go, Kabir."

I get up off the floor and follow him, back into the streets.

Fake Uncle whistles happily, gripping my shoulder as tight as an eagle I saw on TV once, holding on to a squirming mouse.

Except I'm not squirming, because then he'd know I want to escape and he'd get angry. Maybe beat me so much I would limp, just like Aunty Cloud did when the guards punished her for no reason.

Fake Uncle is no better than those guards. Actually, he's worse.

I keep my mouth shut, pretending I heard nothing. But my thoughts aren't silent. They're shouting, *Get away. Soon!*

Maybe I can sneak out of his room when he's asleep—but what if he locks us in and keeps the key close to him?

We pass by a roadside café. Men stand outside, gossiping and sipping hot drinks.

Fake Uncle stops and orders coffee for himself.

*If you need to chuck a stone at someone, do it.* Grandma Knife's words come back to me. What would she do if she were here?

When the waiter puts a cup of frothy coffee on the counter,

Fake Uncle lets go of me. He closes his eyes and takes a deep breath of the bittersweet scent.

I may never get another chance.

For a second, it's like I've split into two, watching one me cheer on another me as I snatch up the cup of steaming hot coffee and fling it in Fake Uncle's face.

Leaving his screams of pain and rage behind, I race out of the shop and away down the street.

# 25

## Parrot Girl

I run as fast as I can and turn a sharp corner. Halfway down an alley, I see a white cow nosing through a huge hill of trash. It's frightening to see a real live animal, but I run toward it, away from Fake Uncle.

A girl with a parrot on her shoulder is strolling toward me. She stops and stares as I close my eyes and dive headfirst into the hill of muck, hoping it'll keep me safe.

I try not to think of all the rotten garbage and who-knows-what-else that's oozing into my nostrils and onto my lips, because I have no choice.

"Hey, girl! Did you see a boy running?" Fake Uncle shouts. His words reach me through the layers of garbage.

"Sure," the girl says. "Yeah."

My heart is hammering so hard, I feel like it's going to shatter my chest. What will he do after he pulls me out of this disgusting rubbish heap?

The girl goes on, "I've seen lots of boys. I've seen lots of girls too!"

"Give me a straight answer or I'll tear out your tongue!" Fake Uncle says.

"Go ahead, sir! Tearing out my tongue will definitely help me tell you what you want to know."

"Will twenty rupees loosen your tongue?"

"Maybe."

"Here! Take this! Which way did he go?"

Did I run from a man who wants to sell me, into the arms of a girl who's going to sell the secret of my hiding place?

"He went that way—see that bus stop down the street?"

"There's no one at the bus stop!"

"That's because people don't stand at bus stops waiting forever," the girl says. "A bus just came by—number 19, I think. You want to find the boy, you better chase him on something other than your feet. He'll be well on his way to the other side of Chennai by now."

# 26

---

# Lost

I'm not sure how long I stay still as a stone with rubbish slithering over me.

"Hey, boy! You getting nice and cozy in there? C'mon out," the girl says. "He's gone."

I crawl out and try to wipe the slime off my eyelids and lips, but my hands and shirt are just as slimy.

"Here!" The girl drops her bag and grabs my chin and wipes my face clean enough so I can see her bright teeth and tangled mass of hair that looks like rusty wire. I guess she's twelve or thirteen—a bit older than me.

"You nearly jabbed my eye," I say, and my voice comes out whinier than I intend. "But, um, thanks!"

"Saved his life, and look what I get. Criticism! What do you think of that, Jay?"

I look around, wondering who Jay is, and see she's talking to the parrot riding on her shoulder. I marvel at its bright green body, curved pink beak, the pink rings around its neck, and its beady eyes. It gazes back at me. Can it really understand her?

"I *am* grateful you saved my life. But you did poke me kind of hard."

"I thought you'd gone off to sleep in there and needed waking up." She grins. "Anyway, here's your money, Prince of Complainers."

"Money?"

"That bully flung some money at me, hoping I'd tell on you. Here," she commands, "take it."

Confused, I extend my palms. They're shaking so much I can hardly keep hold of the money she drops into them.

"Okay! Now get lost."

"I can't get lost," I say. "I mean, I'm already lost."

"Haven't you ever heard that expression before?" Her eyebrows shoot way up. "*Get lost* just means 'go away.' Where did you come from, the moon?"

"Jail." The word pops out of my mouth before I can stop it.

"Jail? You?" She lets her parrot hop onto her wrist and looks at it instead of me. "This little pipsqueak is trying to frighten us, but he has got a lot to learn about lying. Isn't that right, Jay?"

"Rrrright!" It takes me a minute to realize that the parrot is speaking. It has the weirdest voice I've ever heard.

I'm astonished it's saying a word that I can understand. And I'm hurt the girl thinks I lied.

"I did come from jail," I say. "I never lie. And I'm pretty sure you're too brave to get frightened."

"Now he's trying to butter us up, I think." A twinkle pierces her eyes like stars peeping out of the night sky. "Why'd they stick you in jail?"

"I was born there."

"Oh! Your mother is the bad one?"

"No! She's not one bit bad. Some liar accused her of stealing a necklace, and they slammed her behind bars and didn't even try to prove she'd committed a crime."

"Sorry. I shouldn't have accused your mother. That's terrible." The girl pauses, then continues, "Anyway. You better get going."

"Where?"

"Why're you asking me? Do I look like your mother?"

"You don't look anything like her." My mother's face swims into my mind. I miss her so much, it stabs me right in my chest. "Amma's beautiful."

"How nice! I saved you, and now you call me ugly?"

"No, no! I didn't mean that! I just meant you don't look like my mother. Amma is really beautiful when I close my eyes, because her voice is so kind. You're beautiful when my eyes are open, though your voice is kind of mean."

"You should have stopped right after telling me I was beautiful," the girl says. "Even so, what do you think, Jay? Maybe we should let him stay with us, just for tonight?"

She's going to let the parrot decide?

Thankfully, Jay shrieks, "Yes, yes, yes!"

# 27

---

# Cast Out

So," the girl asks as I fall into step beside her, "how'd you escape from jail? Who was the guy chasing you?"

It spills out of me quickly, the whole story of what happened since they released me.

"Such a strange world we live in," she says when I finish. "They lock up nice mothers. But guys who buy and sell kids get to roam free."

I notice passersby wrinkling their noses as they try to avoid getting close to me on the crowded sidewalk. "I need to clean off," I say. "Isn't there anywhere nearby I can wash?"

"Why don't you try that temple?" She points to a small

temple a few feet away with a water tap in the courtyard, where people are rinsing their feet. I run toward it, gazing at the brightly painted sculptures of many-armed gods and goddesses decorating the roof.

"Wait!" she yells. "Don't be silly! Come back!"

What's silly about washing when you're covered in filth? I splash cool water on my face and arms. It feels so good, when suddenly something hard—a pebble!—thuds against my flesh. A man is looking at me the way the guards looked at Mouse Girl when they shoved her in, like I'm the rubbish that's sticking to my skin.

"Get out of here before I throttle you, you low-caste brat!"

"Ai! You leave him alone." The girl is right by me, yelling back at the man. "You touch him and I'll—"

"What'll you do? Call the police?" The man sneers. "You riff-raff. Think you can enter a temple stinking like garbage!"

"You do know you'd have to lay your hands on his low-caste body to throttle him, right?" The girl takes my arm and steers me away while the parrot screeches at the man.

"Thanks," I say once we're down the street. I'm glad she's still holding my arm because I feel like I'll collapse if she lets me go. "You saved my life again."

"Not really. He's the kind of upper-caste snob who'd rather die than touch a low-caste person. But still, I wouldn't do something like that again, because he wouldn't mind whacking you with a stick."

# 28

---

# Caste

So why'd you tell me to wash up in the temple's courtyard if I shouldn't?" I ask the girl. I'm wondering if maybe she's a mixed-up person—some good, some not so good.

"I was joking!" she says. "I thought you knew better than to use a temple's water faucet! Didn't they teach you anything in jail?"

"My teacher taught me a lot. I can sing in different languages, and I know about rivers and butterflies and caterpillars . . ."

"I mean, anything useful?"

"It *is* useful, what I learned!"

"Know how to get food? Know how to get from one place to another? Know a single important thing about surviving?"

"I know you're brave," I blurt out. "That's good. Amma said being brave and kind are the most important things in life."

"You're getting better with the compliments." Her eyes dance, but then she gets all serious. "Do you understand what being low-caste means?"

"Sure. Low-caste means your family cleans bathrooms or does other jobs no one wants. All of us in our cell were low-caste."

"Yes. But now that you're out in the world, you're going to meet high-caste people. Some of them will call you an untouchable. They don't want you anywhere near them if they can help it. And they don't want me either, because I'm Roma."

"What's that?"

"Roma are my people. We have traveled all over the country, hunting and selling beadwork and leather or telling people's fortunes. But wherever we go, people act half fascinated, half scared of us."

"How do people even know your caste?"

"They judge by how I dress and look and speak. I'd fit in easier if I bought a longer skirt and took off my beads and wore my hair differently. But I'm proud of my people. I don't want to hide my caste, do you?"

"Not sure which low caste I even belong to."

"What's your name?"

"Kabir."

"What kind of name is that! I can't even tell your religion by that name, never mind your caste. Are you a Muslim Kabir or a Hindu Kabir?"

"My mother was Hindu and my father was Muslim. So maybe I'm neither one? Or both."

"Better to be both. That way, if you're surrounded by Hindus, say you're Hindu, and if you're surrounded by Muslims, say you're one of them."

"Okay. Anyway, what's your name?"

"You're the first person to ask me my name in about a year." She gives me a big smile. "But I'm fine with that—it's harder to track me down when I'm nameless. Right, Jay?"

"Right, right, right!" the parrot chimes in.

"So, are you going to tell *me* your name?" I ask.

"Sure. My name is Rani, because it means 'queen.' I chose the name myself."

"You named yourself?"

"Yes, so that I could start fresh. I picked a name that shows I can conquer every problem that comes my way."

Rani isn't dressed like a queen, but she holds herself up as proud and tall as I imagine real queens do. I don't know a whole lot about castes and subcastes, but whatever the topmost one is, she looks like she could belong to it.

# 29

---

# Making Plans

Your parrot is amazing," I tell Rani. "Does he understand everything we say?"

"I'm not sure how much he understands." She strokes the top of his head. "He can't carry on a conversation or anything. But parrots can be trained to say lots of human words. He's not the only talking parrot in the world."

"Well, they must be pretty smart if they can speak our language but we can't speak theirs. You're lucky to have him, Rani."

"I am, for sure. But with other things I'm not so lucky. Seems like we both have bad stuff in our lives we want to leave behind, right?"

"I didn't want to leave anything behind." I ignore the parrot's echoes of *right, right.* "I only got out of jail so I can go back."

"That makes no sense, Kabir."

"I mean I want to go back to free my mother."

"How d'you plan to do that?" Rani doesn't sound mean, just curious.

"I—I don't have a plan yet, since I just got out of jail. But I'm hoping I can figure out a way to free Amma somehow."

"D'you know anyone who could help?"

"My father wanted to. He went to Dubai to make money so he could hire us a lawyer."

"So why didn't he rescue you, then?"

"We don't know. He suddenly stopped writing letters a few years ago. But Amma said he was a good man, so if I could just find him . . ."

"Hmmm." Rani chews on her lip. "Kabir, let me tell you something I learned the hard way. Hoping for small stuff you can control is okay. But pinning your hopes on another person is usually a waste of time. Especially if that person is someone who needs to be found."

Rani may know a lot about living in the outside world. But I know a lot about living inside my head—and to keep going, I *need* to keep hoping I can find my father and free Amma.

But as I struggle to keep up with Rani's brisk pace, I start thinking I need to do more than hope.

Rani asked what my plans are, and I need to start making some.

She's right that it'll be hard to find my father. But I know my grandparents live in Bengaluru, so I could try to find them first. Surely my grandparents will help me find Appa, and then he'll pay to get a lawyer to get Amma out of jail.

I can just imagine Amma walking out of that gray building, me holding one of her hands and my father holding the other.

I'm never going to lose hope in that.

# 30

---

## Sweet and Salty Water

I hear a faint whooshing, like a breeze getting stronger and stronger, as we walk along. I keep looking at the sky to see if a storm is coming, until Rani says, "Watch where you're going!" She catches my elbow as I almost stumble into a hole in the sidewalk. "Why're you staring at the sky? Never seen it before?"

"No. I mean, I've never seen so much of it!" I spread my arms out wide and take a moment to enjoy how pretty the sky looks without anything blocking my view. "So much space . . . But it sounds like we might get a storm, doesn't it? Even though the sky is clear?"

"Storm? Oh! You mean the sound of the ocean! I don't suppose you've ever seen the ocean, have you?"

"No," I say. "Just in pictures."

"Well, you're about to see it for real now. The sky, the beach, and the sea."

We turn onto a large road, and Jay whistles happily. "Here we are," Rani says.

I can't take my eyes off the blue stripe of water in the distance. The closer we get, the more incredible it looks. Water tumbling and rolling along, all the way to the edge of the earth. More water than if a thousand taps had been turned on.

In the photos Bedi Ma'am showed us, the ocean looked so peaceful. But this real ocean is a giant snake that never stops hissing.

Rani races ahead, but when I step onto the beach, my feet sink into the sand.

"You scared the sand will swallow your feet, boy?" a man calls out from a fruit stall he's setting up. He chuckles but continues in a kind tone, "Relax. It's not going to hurt you."

Maybe not, but it's strange how the sand keeps shifting under me. I grab a handful and then let it fall through my fingers. It feels so cool and dry, so different from the dirt in the jail yard.

"Come on, Kabir," Rani calls out. I wave to the man and trudge through the sand.

"Want to take a dip?" Rani asks when I join her. She puts her shoulder bag on the sand and sets Jay down on it. Then she takes off her raggedy skirt and runs right into the swooshing ocean in the long, frayed T-shirt she's wearing.

After leaving my slippers next to Rani's things, I stick a toe into the water. It sucks at my feet, but at least the wet sand is firm.

I take another step and then another. I'm in as far as my knees when the sea knocks me off balance with a sudden jerk, sneaking up on me like a bully in the schoolyard. I plop down on my bottom so I'm in water almost to my neck.

"Here." Rani reaches out a hand. "Hold on to me. The waves are just playing with you, Kabir. It's not that rough here today."

Holding on to Rani, who's as firm as a tree rooted in the ground, I feel safer, because the waves feel plenty rough. But I

know I won't get far in this outside world if I'm always clinging to someone. So after a bit, I let go of her and stand on my
own two feet.

"That's right!" Rani encourages. "It's fun, isn't it?"

Slowly, I get used to the rhythm of the waves and feel brave
enough to splash some water on my neck. I scrub at the caked
rubbish so hard it feels like my skin is flaking off, but I'm glad
to be getting cleaner.

Bedi Ma'am said seawater is salty. Maybe it tastes as good as
it feels. As another wave skips up, I gulp in a thirsty mouthful.

Rani laughs as I gag and spit it out. "Didn't you know not to
drink seawater?"

"I—I thought salty water would taste nice, since food usually
tastes better with salt," I sputter.

"Never mind," Rani says kindly. "I bet you're hungry. How
about we go home and I make you a meal with just the right
amount of salt?"

"Thanks," I mumble. I'm glad Rani is still willing to keep me
around, although she must be amazed by my silliness.

# 31

---

# My Self

On the way back to Rani's, we stop at a kiosk shop run by a charity, where a kind woman lets me choose a dry T-shirt. I can't believe it's free, because Bedi Ma'am said I'd have to pay for everything outside. But Rani says you can usually find a few generous people giving away their old clothes.

Next, we visit a public bathroom. I try to walk right in, but Rani stops me. "Only women go into this one. See?" She points at a picture of a woman and then at another doorway, above which I see a picture of a man. "*That's* where you go."

"Oh, sorry. I see now." My brain is already bursting with all the new stuff I've learned, and it's only been one day.

Inside, there's a huge mirror—and the best one I've ever

seen. I yelp when I see my reflection. Not just my face and messy hair, but also my broomstick neck and scrawny body and arms.

I can't stop staring at my reflection. I wave and make faces at myself. I smile and get a great big smile back.

"You okay in there?" Rani calls.

"Yes! Yes, I'm fine," I answer.

"You took a while," Rani says when I come out. "I don't spend a minute longer in there than I must."

"There was this mirror, and it was fun to wave at myself," I say. "Plus this bathroom smells as good as jasmine compared to the one in jail."

"You're easy to please." She grins. "Now let's go home."

"Is it much farther? I've already walked more today than I probably did my whole entire life."

"No—we're almost there." She points ahead. "I live in a tree behind that old estate."

"You live in a tree? Is that because of the parrot?"

Rani laughs. "I live in a tree because it's beautiful—and it doesn't have a mouth, so it can't shout at me to go away."

"Go'way!" Jay calls out. "Go'way, punk!"

"Don't tell me to go away." Rani strokes his bright green back. "I'm the one who looks after you, remember?"

But Jay continues on merrily, adding a string of curse words I recognize from jail.

"Where did he learn that?" I ask.

"From the man who raised him," she says. "I used to call him Grandfather, though he wasn't really family. He had a kind heart but a pretty foul mouth."

"I know how that goes," I say quietly, and my chest squeezes up because her words make me think of Grandma Knife, and that reminds me how far away I am from not only Amma, but also Grandma Knife and Aunty Cloud and Bedi Ma'am and Malli—who are the closest thing I have to family.

# 32

---

# The Tree Home

Rani's tree is a huge, shaggy banyan tree with roots hanging down from its branches.

It's right behind an empty mansion. "People think the house is haunted," she says. "So no one bothers me here."

I'm not sure what *haunted* means, but I don't ask, because I'm sure it's nothing good from the way she says it. It's scary enough with just the two of us being outside now that it's getting dark.

Rani takes a cage out of her bag. Jay hops off her shoulder and onto her wrist.

She feeds him some seeds and then says, "Sleep well, pretty bird."

"Pretty bird," he says, fluffing up his feathers before waddling into the cage. "Pretty birrrd."

Rani scampers up the trunk, climbing one-handed. She hangs the cage on a branch. Jay sticks his head behind his wing.

When Rani gets back on the ground, she takes some matches and things out of her bag. She starts a fire inside a ring of stones and cooks something in a large tin can. When it boils, she takes it off the fire, pours half of it into a smaller can, and gives it to me. It's some kind of stew. I'm so hungry that I hardly chew as I gulp it down and ask for seconds.

"You have a voice like a sparrow but a stomach like a hawk! Here's more. Glad you like it—squirrel stew is my specialty."

"Squirrel?"

"What were you expecting, Prince of Pickiness? Lamb kebab?"

I can feel the stew sloshing around in my stomach. All of a sudden it gushes up, and I clench my lips, but it's like trying to hold back an ocean. I retch and vomit like I'm a tap that can't turn off.

"Ai!" Rani glares at me. "I spent hours trapping and skinning and cooking that squirrel, and you not only eat most of it, but then you throw it all up!"

"I—I'm sorry." I lean against the knobby tree trunk for support. I lie a little so I don't hurt her feelings. "It tasted good—I probably threw up because of all that seawater I swallowed. And how fast I ate."

I dig in my pockets for the money she gave me earlier. The rupee notes are clumped together and damp. "Here. Take this for the food I wasted. If you separate the notes, they'll dry out, I think." I hold them out to her.

"If that's how much you pay for a meal you can't stomach, I wonder what you'd give for one that you find tasty?" Rani pokes at the dying embers of her fire with a stick. "I'm joking. Keep the money. Sorry I got so annoyed."

Looking at Rani, I can see that her anger that swelled up as fast as an ocean wave disappeared just as quickly.

"I'm sorry," I repeat, and I start scuffing dirt over the scattered vomit. "Sorry I messed up your place too."

"Yes, and such a shame, since my maid polished the floor today. But don't worry—we'll be sleeping on the fourth floor, where the air is fresh. I keep the windows open, and the sea breeze blows in through my balcony." Rani's smile sparkles in the moonlight. "Tomorrow, you can buy something to eat with your money. It'll be fun."

Tomorrow! "You mean you don't want me to get lost now?"

"Not right away." Her teasing tone doesn't match the kindness in her eyes. "*I'm* quite happy being alone, because I'm not really alone—I have Jay. But if *you* want to stay, we'll let you. You clearly need our help."

# 33

---

# Outside the Box

Come on." Rani starts climbing her tree. "It's bedtime."

"You sleep up there? Aren't you scared you'll fall?" I feel giddy looking up at Jay's cage, swaying above my head.

"Better in a tree than a room. I could never sleep all shut up like a toy in a box."

"A room isn't a box."

"Yes it is. Anyway, I find the biggest branch and tie myself to the trunk with a rope so I don't fall off. Up here, I'm safe from stray dogs and cats—and humans."

She points at footholds I don't see. I try following her

instructions, but my hands slip and my feet slip and I don't get very far.

"You're kind of weak." Her brows knot together. "But we'll get you in shape soon, don't worry. Tonight, though, why don't you sleep on the ground. Just make sure the jackals don't swallow you up."

I can tell she's joking, but sleep doesn't come easily as I lie all alone beneath the tree. The ground is rougher than the floor in jail. I wiggle around, trying to find a place that doesn't have twigs poking into my back.

The night is full of weird sounds too. Jail wasn't quiet, but at least I knew where the noises came from. And my skin prickles when a breeze wafts over me. Even though part of me knows that fresh air is better than a hot, stuffy cell, I wish I were back there. I wish I were with Amma.

I miss Amma so much and know she must be missing me too.

But I'm sure she's being brave, like I need to be. Or at least I need to do something to stop the sea of tears that's threatening to rush down my cheeks.

So I start to sing. At first my voice trembles like the leaves over my head, but then the song strengthens it. I pretend my voice can carry all the way to where Amma can hear it.

From somewhere in the branches above me, I hear Rani say sleepily, "You have a nice singing voice, Kabir."

Her words are a gift, bringing a tiny smile to my face. Then she sends another gift: A ragged old sheet comes floating down. "You can put that over your head if it makes you feel better."

Hidden under the sheet, I do feel better. Safe enough to sink into a strange dream where I'm bobbing up and down in a stormy ocean that carries me far away from Amma.

# 34

## A String of Pearls

The sun pokes at my eyes and wakes me up. It's strange to have no one sleeping anywhere near me—no Amma, no Grandma Knife or Aunty Cloud. I even almost miss Mouse Girl.

I wonder what they'll do today without me—if Malli will be scared to walk past the punishment block on her own and what Bedi Ma'am will teach. Right now, Amma'll be lining up to use the bathroom.

Here, at least, I don't need to wait for someone to unlock a door to let me pee.

I find a nearby tree to hide behind, and I go! *The whole world is my toilet now,* I want to sing. This is what freedom feels like.

In the sunshine, the rustling leaves don't sound scary at all. Birds and squirrels and monkeys chatter merrily in the abandoned garden. Then Rani's voice floats down and joins the chorus. Much nicer sounds to start the day with than the jail noises—sliding bolts, squeaking keys, rattling locks.

Rani stops singing. "Up at last, sleepyhead?"

"Please, won't you sing some more?"

"I wasn't singing, really, just chanting my family's names."

"Your family name is long enough for a song?" Mine's so short. One syllable. Khan.

"Not just one name. I was reciting the names of my ancestors, going back ten generations."

"Ten generations? Oh wow!" And I don't even know my own grandparents' first names.

"We don't have much else to carry," she says. "Other people have money and things, but these are the pearls Roma women carry, these strings of names."

"Will you sing it again? You have a nice voice, nicer even than the birds," I say as a crow starts cawing.

"I sound better than a crow?" She throws back her head and laughs. "I have some advice for you, Prince of Compliments: You better think a little harder before you open your mouth, or else you'll be Prince of Insults and might get in trouble."

Rani sings the names again, and I hear longing in her voice. She must miss her mother as much as I miss mine. In jail, Amma taught me never to pester anyone about their past, but a question slips out of me before I can stop it. "Why're you alone, Rani?"

"Alone? Don't be silly. I'm with Jay, can't you see?"

She snatches up his cage so forcefully the parrot wakes up, screeching, "Ai! Ai! Ai!"

"Just me," she says to Jay. "Hush now, so I can get breakfast."

Still up in the branches, she fits a stone from her waist pouch into a thick Y-shaped stick with a leather belt. She aims at a crow and pulls the belt back. It twangs. The stone flies, and the crow thuds to the ground.

"You killed it! Why?"

"Breakfast," she says.

Rani plucks the bird and orders me to collect branches for her fire. I'm happy to because then I don't have to look at the dead crow. And I'm even happier when she doesn't force me to eat it.

"Luckily for you, there are fruit trees in this garden," she says. She pelts stones at a tree with small, dark leaves, and bunches of a long brown fruit fall to the ground. "Try a tamarind." She shows me how to peel off the hard skin and suck on the sweet-sour flesh inside.

The tamarinds aren't very filling, but I don't complain. After all, I'm used to having a half-empty stomach from mornings in jail.

From another tree, she picks a fat guava, which tastes sweet and delicious. As I lick the sticky pink juice off my fingers, she laughs. "Wish you could see yourself now, Prince of Dribblers. Let's go visit your mirror so you can wash your face."

# 35

## Fortune-Telling

We leave Rani's tree behind and visit the public bath-room. Rani doesn't have tooth powder, but she shows me how to brush my teeth with a fresh twig from a neem tree. It tastes so bitter, I want to vomit again, but at least there's enough water for me to rinse out the bad taste.

"Now I need to go to work," Rani says. "You want to come?"

"Yes, please." I don't want to return to the noisy part of the city, but I need to get used to it if I'm going to search for my grandparents.

Soon, we're plunging through rivers of traffic. Rani holds one of my hands and guides me through the blaring vehicles. I narrow my eyes, focusing only on her and Jay, who's riding on her shoulder as unruffled by the commotion as she is, and we finally make it to the other side.

"Here!" she says, settling down in a patch of shade cast by a wall at the corner of two busy roads.

This spot feels so open and unprotected. What if Snake Man or Fake Uncle finds me? I hug my knees to my chest and try burying my head behind them. I wish I had wings so I could hide my head like Jay does when he's sleeping.

"Kabir?" Rani says. "It's a huge city and we're nowhere near where I found you yesterday." She fingers her waist pouch, which bulges with stones. "And my slingshot is right here. Trust me. I won't let anyone catch you."

Her confidence reassures me a little.

Rani sets cards out on the sidewalk. I pick one up. It has Tamil words written on it.

"You play games with people?" I ask. I hope she doesn't gamble, the way I've seen some women do with cards in jail. "My teacher said gambling was a very bad thing to do."

"Don't worry. I just help people who are scared or worried.

Watch." She starts chanting, "May I tell your fortune? Step up, and me and my wise parrot will tell you what the future holds!"

"Step up, step up, step up," Jay chimes in every now and then.

"Can you really tell the future?"

"Other people think we have magic powers, which is what's important," Rani says.

"*Do* you have any magic powers?" Maybe Rani can make jail guards sleep and help set my mom free, like in the Krishna story.

"Aiyo." She rolls her eyes. "If I had magic powers, why would I hunt crows for breakfast?"

She starts chanting again as passersby jostle along the crowded sidewalk. Most of them barely glance at us, but eventually, an old man shuffles up, adjusts his dusty white turban, and leans on his cane. "You can tell me something for ten rupees?"

"Yes! Of course, Master-ji!" Rani gives him a dazzling smile.

"How do you know I'm a teacher?" The old man looks impressed.

"The spirits give me clues." Rani's voice gets deeper. "I know, Master-ji, that you are a great teacher . . . you teach language . . . Hindi."

"Very good. All correct." Master-ji sounds as pleased as Bedi Ma'am when I did well on a test. "What else can you tell me?"

"For twenty, I can tell you twice as much, and for fifty—"

"If I still had fifties to give away, I wouldn't be standing on a street corner, asking you to tell my future."

"Okay, Master-ji. Ten. Come and help me see the future, Jay!" Rani holds out her hand, and Jay hops onto it from her shoulder and then onto the ground near the cards she has laid out. "What do the spirits say for Master-ji?"

Jay pecks at one of the cards. Rani picks it up and reads it. Her whole body shudders. Her eyes roll. "I see . . . I see . . . sunshine, like gold, shimmering! Money will come your way, yes, Master-ji, it will indeed, but—wait—beware! The card says beware a man . . ."

"A young mustached man?" the old grandfather suggests.

"A thin, gleaming mustache and scheming, greedy eyes," Rani declares.

"You must be seeing my son," the man says. "He's always asking me for money. I wish he'd get a job and stop pestering me. Will he get a job, can you tell?"

"He will get a job sooner if you stop giving him your money. Be firm, Master-ji."

"Quite right," the old man says. "I'll speak to him sternly. Anything else I can do?"

"Place a pinch of sacred ash from the temple on your turban every morning, and as you do so, remind yourself that you must be firm with him."

"Ash? In my turban?" The man twirls his cane between his fingers. "Never heard of such a thing. Still, I suppose that is easy enough to do . . ."

"There is a harder thing," Rani mumbles.

"Tell me," the man says eagerly.

"Kindness today, this very hour—give generously to those who are not your family, and your generosity will reap a reward more magnificent than you can dream!"

"Okay, okay," the man says. "Here's fifteen, and if that lazy son of mine gets a job soon, I'll come back and give you and your pretty bird more."

"Pretty bird, pretty bird!" Jay trills as the man hobbles away.

# 36

---

## Stories and Songs

How did you know that man teaches Hindi?" I ask.

"A lucky guess? No, really, I've seen him before—carrying textbooks and papers. Plus he always visits the temple after school, and once I heard a boy in a school uniform complaining that 'Master-ji' gave him a bad mark on his Hindi test. Then he practically ran into Master-ji and almost dropped dead. Clearly, he was worried his teacher had heard him. As for the old man's Tamil, he speaks with an accent, so he must have moved here from somewhere else."

"What about the rest? About his future?" I ask eagerly. "The card didn't say a word about ash in turbans. How did you know it would bring Master-ji luck?"

"You can read? You said you were born behind bars."

"They had a school in jail. I had a nice teacher called Bedi Ma'am."

"My mother always wanted me to go to school," Rani says wistfully. Then she grins. "Maybe I should try jail school, since they won't want me anywhere else."

This must be another joke, but I don't find it funny. "So you lied? Lying is wrong!"

Rani shrugs. "The way I look at it, there's nothing wrong with making things. Or selling things you make. Right? I made up a story and sold it. You think storytellers are liars?"

"No, storytelling is fine. My mother told stories. But that wasn't a story," I insist. "You were pretending to know what's going to happen to Master-ji."

"I wasn't pretending, I was guessing, and I am pretty good at it because I observe people. I pay attention to the way they wiggle their mouths and eyes and arms and feet and how they walk and stand."

I suppose that's not so different from Amma, who could see from people's faces right into their hearts. Most of the time, at least.

"I try to guess their dreams and give them hope, Kabir. What's wrong with hopes and dreams?"

"But they expect what you tell them will actually happen!"

"If they're expecting things, then it's their fault. They're grown-ups—they should know that expecting life to give them something isn't smart."

I wish Amma were around to tell me what is and isn't smart. Everything out here is so confusing. Smells stab my nose— fumes from the road, rotting food from a garbage bin, and others I don't recognize. My ears hurt from the endless noise of traffic. I sit miserably beside Rani for a while, and then I start singing a song softly, to comfort myself.

To my surprise, two women slow down to listen to me, and when I'm done, they drop money on the ground beside me.

"Now, isn't this a wonderful way to earn money!" Rani dusts off the coins. "Your pockets will be jingling by the end of the day! See that tree at the end of the street with the fiery orange blossoms? That's called a gulmohur tree. Go and sit under it and sing, and come back when you're tired."

I hesitate because I'm afraid to leave Rani's side.

"Don't worry," she says, reading my mind. "I'll keep an eye on you."

I can't stop worrying, but I walk to the tree anyway. Sitting under the gulmohur tree, I start singing my favorite songs.

I marvel at the women walking past who all wear such beautifully colored saris and make me feel as if I'm sitting in a rainbow. Every once in a while, someone tosses coins in my direction. By the time the sun is at the center of the sky, I have a shiny hill of coins.

I pick up the coins one by one, turning them around, holding them up and watching how the sun glints off them. I listen to the way they clink and jostle together as I fill my pocket with them.

"Money! Money! Money!" I start singing. "Thank you, God up in the sky."

# 37

———

# Money

My happiness over my pile of money is cut short.

Someone taps my shoulder from behind. I whip around.

"Hand over the money, kid." It's a teenager with arms as thick as tree trunks. "Now!"

I try to raise my voice and cry, "Help!" but all that comes out is a froglike croak. Where's my voice when I need it most? Where's Rani? I can't see her anywhere.

The bully holds open a plastic bag and orders, "Drop your money in this. Quick."

My whole body shakes. Just as I reach into my pocket,

something whizzes past my head and strikes the bully's shoulder, making him yelp.

Then a voice starts shrieking, "Go'way, punk. Go'way!"

The teenager's eyes bulge at the sound of Jay, who's screeching curses from somewhere above us. The kid takes a quick, frantic look around and then races away.

Rani shinnies down the tree and lands beside me.

"I never saw you climb up there!" My voice is shaky, but at least it's working again. "You hit him?"

"Me? No, no. An invisible angel chased him away." She laughs, but I can't.

"Thanks for saving me. Again. I should've known better."

"Don't worry. It was the first time you earned money. No wonder you were too excited to think what you were doing."

"I was inviting someone to steal from me, singing about my money." I bite my lip.

"Ai!" Rani catches hold of my shoulders and gives me a little shake. "Never blame yourself for someone else's cruelty. My mother always said there's enough people waiting to accuse us falsely without us doing it to ourselves. Isn't that right, Jay?"

"Right," Jay chirps. "Right. Right. Rrriiight!"

"Anyway, we all have a lot to learn." Rani shrugs. "Everyone makes mistakes."

"You don't. You're like a hero in a movie. Always saving everyone."

"Not really." She stares at a bus lurching across the road. "I couldn't save my family."

Rani opens her mouth and closes it without saying anything. It looks like she can't decide whether to tell me more. Jay nips her ear as if he's encouraging her, and she finally speaks. "A few years ago, my family and I were camped near a village. The rains never came that year, and there was a drought. The villagers blamed us. Said we brought bad luck. Told us we had to go."

She takes a breath and then plunges into the rest of her story. "It got worse. When we didn't leave, the villagers tried to kill us all, and the police wouldn't help." Her voice falters, and she pauses, then continues in almost a whisper, "My father died. Only my mother and I escaped by hiding in a cave. We ran away and went to live with my uncle's family. The problem was that he wanted to marry me off when I turned fourteen. So I ran away before that could happen. With my mother's blessing—and help."

We start walking along. I open my mouth but shut it again, just like Rani did before telling me her story. Except now I keep mine shut tight.

Rani and I are both on our own. Far away from mothers we love. My life hasn't been easy. But hers sounds even worse.

# 38

---

# Tasting a Piece of Sky

Hungry?" Rani asks, changing the subject. "What do you like best to eat?"

"Laddus." My empty stomach twists so hard it hurts. My heart hurts worse, imagining Rani's pain—but I sense she doesn't want to talk about her past anymore.

"Expensive taste," Rani says. "But we definitely need to get some food."

My feet, blistered from all the walking, hurt as much as my hungry stomach. At least I'm wearing chappals on my feet. Rani isn't, but the soles of her bare feet look tougher than my slippers—rougher even than Amma's feet.

The traffic is slower in this hottest part of the afternoon, but horns still blast, and buses still belch smoke. Heat curls in the air above the shiny tar road.

We come to a stop at last in front of a pushcart with a stove on it.

Rani points to the man snoozing next to it. "This grandpa isn't the best cook," Rani says, "but he's nice and doesn't chase away low-caste kids. Choose what you want from the menu."

"Menu?"

"The list of food." She points at the blackboard propped against the wheel of the man's pushcart, with a long list of items scribbled on it.

I read the menu. And reread it.

"Well?" Rani says. "Can you read or can't you?"

"Yes, but—I've never had so many choices. Actually . . . I've never had any choices. In jail they just decided what we could eat. And wear. And even when we could go to the bathroom."

"Well, luckily you're not there anymore!"

"I don't even know what most of the choices are. You choose. You choose for me, Rani."

"Okay, but next time you'll decide. Please, sir," Rani calls loudly. "May we have some soan papdi?"

The old man doesn't seem to mind that we woke him up.

The two of them bargain. Rani finally agrees on a price, and the man fills a plastic bag with something flaky and yellow. She gives me a piece to taste.

"Mmm . . ." It tastes like a cloud that has floated down to earth, airy and sweet, melting on my tongue. "This is even better than laddus."

"Cheaper too." Rani grins. "Sometimes I work in the evenings, but you look like you need rest, so I'll ask the boss if I can take a holiday. Can we go home, Jay?"

"Yes! Yes! Yes!" Jay agrees.

"Does he ever say no to you?" I ask.

"Only if I want him to. I give him cues with my head. If I move my head down just a tiny bit like this and turn up my lips like this, he'll say yes. If I tilt my head like this instead, when I ask him a question, he'll say no."

That means, the first day we met, Rani made Jay say yes so that I could stay with them. She wanted me as a friend right from the beginning. That thought keeps me going as I trudge behind her.

# 39

---

# Buying a Plane

Before we get back to the tree, Rani stops again to buy some dried fish and some other food from vendors sitting on the sidewalk, selling things in baskets.

Rani insists I should also taste a sort of fizzy water that she calls a goli soda.

"My favorite drink," she says. "Isn't it good?"

"Yes," I lie. It is nice to have something cool rushing down my throat, but the bursting bubbles make me feel like little frogs are leaping around inside my mouth.

"I'm glad you've found a good way to earn so soon," Rani says, back at the tree. "Singing isn't that different from telling stories, is it?"

"Isn't it?"

"My stories make people happy. Your songs make people happy. Happy people share their money so that other people can make their stomachs happy."

"That's true, I guess. Do you spend all your money on food?"

"Mostly. Sometimes I get seeds or special treats for Jay. Why? You want to buy something?"

"What if—what if I bought a plane? Then I could fly to Bengaluru to find my grandparents, and then we could fly to Dubai, and they could help me find my father, and then we could save Amma."

"You have a better chance of sprouting wings on your back than saving enough for a plane ticket, let alone a plane."

"My teacher told me a little bit about tickets, but I sort of forgot. And I guess I should know that only rich people own planes."

"It's okay, Kabir. You're doing pretty well for someone who just got out of jail. So, planes are expensive. There are cheaper ways to travel than flying. Trains don't cost as much, especially third class. Bus tickets are cheap too. But I've never heard of Dubai, and if it's far away, even bus and train tickets will be super expensive. Plus, remember what I said about pinning your hopes on your father?"

I ignore her last question. "I can at least save for a bus or train ticket to Bengaluru, right? It's close by. I saw it on a map once. Or maybe I could even walk there . . ." As I say this, I think about the blisters on my feet that make them look as bubbly as the soda we drank. But no matter how badly my feet might hurt, I want to start searching for my family as soon as I can.

"Bengaluru isn't *that* close. It's in another state. When I lived with my family, we traveled a lot, so I know." She laughs, but sadly. "And no way you could walk there. Plus, in Bengaluru, people speak another language."

"No problem! I speak that language. My mother comes from there, so she taught me. And she showed me a picture of the mosque where my father worshipped, called the Juma Masjid. I learned all about it! My teacher said it was built by the great Tipu Sultan, out of a smooth white stone called marble."

"You really do want to find out what happened to your dad, don't you?" Rani says. "I suppose I would feel the same way if I were you."

"My father told Amma that he looked just like my grandfather.

And Amma said I look exactly like my father, so that means I look like my grandfather too. And their last name is Khan, like mine."

"Those are all good clues, Kabir." Her forehead scrunches up. She seems to be thinking hard about something. Then she announces, "Let's go to the mosque and find your family! Let's go to Bengaluru."

"You'll come with me? Really?"

"Sure. If we work for a while longer, we can save enough to go there together."

"That's great. I'll feel much better having you with me," I confess. "You're so smart and brave. We're kind of opposite. You know the names of ten ancestors, and I don't even know my grandparents' first names. You love sleeping under the sky, but I'm scared to sleep without a roof. You know so much and I know so little."

"You learn fast, though," she says. "Like me. Right, Jay?"

"Right," Jay chirps in agreement. "Right, right, right."

# 40

---

# Caged

"Step up!" Jay's high-pitched voice reaches me from the other end of the street.

Resting my back against the gulmohur tree, I watch him and Rani at work. Jay struts up and down before he pecks at a card, while a woman waits to hear Rani tell her fortune.

Despite the tree's shade and the breeze, I'm sweating. But at least the air is moving out here. With the weather getting hotter, I worry about how Amma and the others are doing, and if the fan is working. I miss her so much, my throat squeezes up and I can't breathe, let alone sing.

Except I don't have a choice. So I try to shove my sadness down as deep as I can by imagining I'm holding Amma's hand and leading her out of jail. I imagine hard, until I can sing in a voice that's strong and happy.

The kind of voice that customers pay to hear.

I get lots of visitors—a few of whom pay even without listening to a whole song. I feel quite pleased with myself until Rani tells me she told everyone who asked her for their fortune that they'd do well if they were generous to poor boys.

That night, I eat Rani's squirrel stew without complaining, although it still makes my stomach queasy. But the less money we spend on food, the more we'll save.

Rani lets Jay sit on my shoulder for a bit before we settle in for the night. I love the feel of his tiny feet digging into my shoulder. Just a little, but not enough to hurt. And I love it when he ruffles his feathers and they tickle my cheeks. And when he gives my ear a playful nip.

"How did you find Jay?" I ask.

"I think I told you about the old man who was like a grandfather to me, right? He was the first person I met when I came to the city. When he saw me, he said he'd tell my fortune for free. I said I didn't care what was going to happen, because I already knew it couldn't be anything good.

"He proved me wrong. He shared his food with me and sort of adopted me. He taught me how to read the cards and tell stories. After he died, Jay was the only family I had left, and we made this tree our home because no one bothers us here."

"This tree isn't a proper home, though, is it?" I ask. "I mean, it won't protect us when the rains come. Amma said a home is a nice place—a house with rooms—"

"Fine. If your mother says that proper homes have to have rooms and roofs, then you go build one, Kabir," Rani snaps.

"Sorry. I didn't mean it's not nice here. It's just—I'm still scared to sleep out in the open."

"I shouldn't have been mean about your mother." Rani's anger only ever seems to last for a minute or two. "But I don't think you need a roof to make a home. My people's favorite roof is the sky." Rani picks Jay up off my shoulder and sets him in front of his cage. "Sleep well, pretty bird."

"Pretty bird," Jay says to himself, waddling into this cage. "Pretty, pretty, pretty bird."

I hate the sound of the cage door snapping shut. "Does he have to go in a cage? It reminds me of jail."

"It's not a jail to him," she says. "He likes it, and the bars protect him from other animals. Bars aren't just for locking people up, you know. Lots of people have bars on their windows to protect their stuff, because they're scared other people will steal."

I think about the tall wall around the house where Amma and Appa worked. All the mansions in that neighborhood had iron grilles on the windows. Funny to think rich people, who can be free, build fancy cages to live in. Probably because they're afraid of poor people like us.

And not so funny to think how they're so afraid that they lock up innocent people like Amma. My heart clenches as tightly as a fist when I think about how much she's suffered. How much she's *still* suffering every single day.

# 41

## Like the Moon

Even though my throat feels sore from singing, our pile of money has hardly grown in the last few days.

"By the time we save enough for a ticket, I'll have a long white beard," I call up to Rani as I shift uncomfortably on the ground.

"Stop complaining and sing us a song, Prince of Worriers!" she calls.

So I sing her the lullaby about the moon, the one Amma sang to me my last night in jail, but it makes me miss her so much, I choke up and can't even finish the second verse.

"What's wrong?" Rani asks.

It's too hard to talk about Amma, so I say, "How are we ever going to find my grandparents? Cities are so full of people. Isn't it going to be impossible?"

"No. We have lots of great clues, and we're going to follow them. Your mosque is a big one. We follow it and see where it leads. Come on. Finish the song."

I do my best. When I'm done singing, Rani says, "You're so funny, Kabir. You sing about the moon and you don't see what it does? It never gives up."

"What do you mean, the moon never gives up?"

"Each month it gets whittled away and has to start from nothing and build itself up again. It returns, full and shiny, every month. You shouldn't give up either."

I wonder if Amma's lullaby about the moon climbing over mountains to bring us flowers was a message about how the moon never gives up too.

I wish I'd asked her if the words had an inner meaning, the way some of the poems Bedi Ma'am taught me did.

I wish I knew when I'll be able to speak to Amma again.

# 42

---

# Falling Stars

The weather's getting hotter and hotter, and my skin is sticky with sweat when I wake up. I drink all the water in my plastic bottle, but I'm still thirsty. If it's so unbearably hot out in the open, I don't want to think how awful it must be inside the jail.

When we go to the public bathroom to wash up, not a drop of water comes out of the faucet.

An old man entering the bathroom after me shakes his head when I tell him there's no water. "Surprise, surprise," he says. "First thing they do when there's water scarcity is turn it off in places where people like us live."

"There's a water pump not too far away," Rani says, and we head over to it and join the line of people hoping to fill their water bottles. I do my best to freshen up, though I figure I'm going to sweat more anyway.

Before I start my first song, a rich-looking woman glides by. She looks right through me, the way passersby usually do, as if I'm no bigger than the beetle crawling in a crack in the sidewalk. Her earrings flash like daytime stars. They're golden and dangly, set with tiny red stones, and I've never seen anything like them. They sparkle as she runs a hand over her shiny black braid—and then I notice, with a shock, that an earring is coming off.

For a moment it's caught in her hair, and then it falls onto the pavement, but she doesn't notice.

Rani watches as I leap up and snatch the fallen earring before anyone can step on it. I close my fist over it.

The earring is surely worth more than two train tickets. But I promised Amma I'd make her proud. More than anything, Amma wanted me to be good.

"Ma'am! Ma'am!" I chase after the woman, but she keeps on pretending she can't see or hear me.

"Ma'am?" Rani catches up to us and plants herself right in the woman's tracks. "You may not see us, but we saw your earring fall off, and my friend rescued it."

The woman actually meets our eyes at last. She gives us an embarrassed smile when I dangle the earring in front of her. "Oh my goodness!" she says. "I can't believe it! I'll never go back to that jeweler. It cost me— Thank you. Thank you both, so much."

She puts her earring in her purse and sighs. "I'm sorry I ignored you both. It's just there are so many poor kids in this city. This country. This world. You have to look away. You understand, don't you?" Her pleading eyes gaze into mine. "If only the whole world were filled with people as honest as you, we'd be better off."

"Thanks, ma'am."

"No, no. I need to thank you. Anything you'd like me to get for you? Clothes? Food?"

"We don't need anything from you." Rani marches away.

"Wait! I'm sorry," the woman cries. "I'm really sorry!" She turns to me. "I'm so grateful for your honesty. Please let me give you something."

Rani stops, turns around, and looks at me. I guess she thinks it's my decision.

"Please?" the woman begs again. "It would make me feel so much better if I could help you a little."

Rani may be too angry to take anything from the woman, but I'm not that proud.

"Money for us to travel to Bengaluru by train." I hope it's not too much to ask for.

The woman's eyes brighten with relief. She reaches into her purse and pulls out more money than I've ever seen in my whole life. "Great, here you go."

"Thank you, ma'am!"

"Thank you," Jay trills. "Thank you."

For a moment I'm scared Rani is still irritated with the woman, but as always, Rani's anger bubble has floated away. She runs over, looking as excited as I feel.

# 43

---

# Calling the Police

Can we leave for Bengaluru right now?" I ask.

"No, I have to ask my boss for permission first." Rani grins. "Of course we can!"

Jay catches our excitement and whistles happily. We return to the tree, where Rani converts the sheet I sleep on into a kind of sling and bundles our few things into it.

Rani knows the way to the station, so all I have to do is follow her, which is a good thing, since my brain feels all fuzzy, as if I'm dreaming. By the time we reach the station, my whole body has turned into a sort of cloud. But I come down to earth when Rani tries to buy us a ticket.

"We don't let your kind on our trains," the man at the ticket counter announces. "You stink so much, your whole compartment will empty out."

"We don't stink!" I'm angrier than ever, but my voice surprises me, bursting out so fierce and strong. "You sell us our train tickets or else—"

"Or else what? You'll call the police?" The man laughs.

A wiry old man interrupts us. "What's the problem here?"

"We did nothing wrong!" I exclaim.

"Exactly. I saw that you did nothing wrong. But this fellow did." He steps up to the counter. "You sell those children a ticket. Right now."

"Who are you, mister? The prime minister?" The man sneers.

"Mr. Subramaniam, retired Indian Police Service officer. And if you don't believe me, I'll just call one of my former colleagues, and they'll bring a pair of very fine bracelets made especially for your wrists."

The ticket man's face twitches like he's been stung. "I was going to give them a ticket, sir. It was just a joke, sir."

"I don't share your sense of humor," Mr. Subramaniam says.

"Next train to Bengaluru is the Brindavan Express, leaving in a few minutes." The nasty ticket man is all polite to us now. "Or you want the overnight mail train? Or—"

Brindavan! My heart skips when I hear the name of the next train. It feels lucky. Brindavan, in Amma's story, is where Lord Krishna spent his childhood.

Mr. Subramaniam watches over us as we buy our tickets, but I still double-check the change. Bedi Ma'am warned me to be careful, after all.

"You'll be all right in Bengaluru?" Mr. Subramaniam asks. "Someone will meet you there?"

"My grandparents live there, sir." I avoid telling the truth, but avoid lying too.

His eyes flicker over me and over Rani, as if he can tell there's more to our story—but he doesn't ask any more questions. Instead he says, "My childhood wasn't easy because I wasn't rich, but it helped that I wasn't an outcaste. I'm sorry people treat kids like you so badly."

He guides us through the crowded platform to the train to make sure we get on safely.

"Be careful," he says as we thank him. "Right now is a bad time for Tamil-speaking kids to travel to Bengaluru. Tension is running higher than usual between our two states, with everyone arguing about how to share water. And lots of men are just looking for an excuse to fight and take out their anger on anyone, even a kid."

# 44

## Saint Kabir's Song

Rani puts Jay in his cage, hands him to me, and then insists on sitting by the open door of the carriage.

"You're going to fall out!" I say.

"You know I hate being inside boxes. I'm going to see if I can ride on top of the roof."

"No you're not." A man in a khaki uniform strides in. "You fall on the tracks, it'll be my job on the line."

"Are you a policeman, sir?" I ask.

"Sort of," he says. "I check if you have tickets, and if not, I throw you off the train."

I remember what Bedi Ma'am said about conductors as I whip our tickets out of my pocket. The man punches holes in them and moves on.

Rani chooses a seat next to an open window and sticks a hand out of it as if she needs to hold on to the fresh air. I sit in between Rani and an old woman whose hair shines like moonlight on the ocean.

A loud whistle blows, and the train jerks forward. Sitting in a moving train feels as strange to me as when I sat in the police van. I clutch the bottom of the seat with one hand and put my other hand over Jay's cage to keep it from sliding around.

"Pretty bird you've got there," the old woman remarks.

"Pretty, pretty, pretty bird," Jay informs her before sticking his head behind his wing for a snooze.

"Very pretty." She laughs. "What's your name, son?"

"Kabir, Aunty," I say politely. In my head, I name her Aunty Silver for her silvery hair.

A burly man sitting across from us butts in, "Kabir like a Muslim, or Kabir like a Hindu?"

"Why do you care?" Rani turns away from the window for a moment to glare at him.

The man looks muscular enough to haul her out onto the tracks. Hoping to avoid a fight, I say quickly, "Saint Kabir. You know, the one who wrote songs."

I sing one of Saint Kabir's songs, and then, since the man probably doesn't understand the words, I explain what it means, just the way Bedi Ma'am explained it to me: that people of all religions are equal, and God thinks caste is a cruel human invention.

The rest of the people in the cramped compartment clap when I'm done, but Muscle Man just says, "Well, seeing as you are not a saint, I think it's all right for me to ask your caste."

"Why do you care about his religion? Or their caste?" Aunty Silver demands. "Leave the poor kids alone!"

"Why do *you* care about them?" Muscle Man growls at Aunty Silver.

"Ai, she's old enough to be your mother. Speak to her with respect!" a young man says, jumping into the quarrel. "Don't you stingy Bengaluru people know better than to use that rude tone when you address your elders?"

"Who are you calling stingy?" Muscle Man raises his voice. "We give you Tamil people more of our river's water than we keep for ourselves."

"It's our river too!" the young man counters. "And we're careful with our water, while you people waste it!"

Muscle Man shakes his fist at the nice young man. I wish Grandma Knife were here to break up the argument, like I've seen her do with angry women in jail.

I try to catch Rani's eye, but she's gazing out the window as if her life depends on it and she doesn't care what's happening inside. She's putting up with so much discomfort for my sake. I feel very lucky I found her.

And when I glance at the men again, I feel a little bit lucky that they're so busy arguing with each other that Muscle Man is leaving me in peace.

Soon, everyone in the compartment joins in the argument, agreeing with the young man, and Muscle Man backs off.

"Rest, boy," Aunty Silver says. "I'll keep an eye out for you."

I lean back, close my eyes, and pretend I'm asleep. What a mixed-up world. Bedi Ma'am was right—adults are terrible at sharing. They are even *worse* than the boys in jail school.

# 45

---

# Bengaluru

The train rocks me to sleep. But then it suddenly jerks and wakes me again. Muscle Man is snoring, and the young man who argued with him is chatting quietly with someone else. Jay's head is still hidden behind his wing, and Rani has finally nodded off too.

"Awake? Want an idli?" Aunty Silver offers me a fluffy white rice cake, which tastes like a salty cloud. "I made them myself."

"They taste better than anything I've eaten," I mumble through a mouthful. "You're a great cook, Aunty."

Aunty Silver gives me a few idlis for Rani when she wakes up, and I continue to gobble up as many as I can stuff into my stomach.

"When I was young, we always had rain," Aunty Silver says, motioning out the window at a stretch of cracked earth. "Fields were greener than your parrot's wings. But the weather has been changing. Every year it gets hotter. The monsoon fails. Rivers run dry. Water gets scarce, and there isn't enough food to go around. And when your stomach is empty, it's easy to fill your soul with rage and start fighting for no good reason with other innocent people."

"The ground does look thirsty," I agree, looking out at the landscape, full of straggly plants and trees with withered leaves.

After a while, buildings start sprouting up outside the window, and soon we're entering a city with buildings that are even taller than the ones in Chennai city.

When, at last, the train chugs into the Bengaluru station, Aunty Silver warns us, just like Mr. Subramaniam did, "Be careful. And good luck!" Then she hops off the train and disappears into the noisy sea of people on the platform.

Porters leap into action to help rich passengers with their luggage as we exit the train. They're wearing red uniforms, just as in Chennai, and they're bargaining just as loudly with the passengers, but in Kannada!

The secret language I used to speak with just Amma in jail is spoken everywhere here. I love how it sounds.

The crowd of people pushes us along, but I stop when we enter the station to soak it all in. Rani tugs at me and shouts, "Come on!" But her voice gets a little wobbly when she asks, "Hmm . . . how're we going to find the mosque?"

"I'll ask someone."

"You will? How?"

"My parents grew up in this city, remember? My mother and I always talked in Kannada—especially when we didn't want others listening to us in jail."

But asking someone isn't so easy. No matter whom I address or how respectfully, none of the people stop. It's as if we're see-through, and it doesn't even help when I get Jay to sit on my finger.

Finally, I walk over to a bent old man who sits cross-legged on the floor, begging. I wave a coin in front of the man's face as I ask him my question. He answers, and as I let the coin tinkle onto his plate, I feel proud. In this city where Rani doesn't speak the language, I'm the most useful member of our two-person-plus-one-bird team.

# 46

---

# At the Mosque

The mosque sits firm as a rock, rising above the river of noise and movement rushing around it. It's as beautiful as the picture Appa drew for Amma, but much grander than the photo Bedi Ma'am showed me.

"How easily we found your family's mosque!" Rani says, her eyes gleaming with excitement. "Now we just sit and watch everyone who enters or leaves that gate!"

"But there's a million people here!" I say. "Even if my grandfather actually comes by, how will I ever know it's him?"

"Aiyo!" Rani rolls her eyes. "Didn't you say your mother said you looked like him?"

"Yes—but I'm not sure what I'd look like if I had a gray beard and my face was all wrinkly."

"Leave that part to me, Prince of Panic. I'm good at recognizing faces."

"Okay, then how about you look at the people, and I sing?" I suggest.

I don't feel like singing, but I realize if I want to eat something more than squirrel stew, it's up to me to earn cash now. Rani can't speak Kannada, so she can't tell anyone's fortune in this city.

The cool white marble of the mosque glows in the late-afternoon sunlight. I fix my eyes on it to soothe the worries wriggling around in my head. We take up our positions on either side of the gate in the square that surrounds the mosque. It's much nicer than sitting on a roadside pavement.

Rani eats the idlis I saved for her while Jay whistles as if he's enjoying himself. I look up hopefully at every passerby, but after what seems like hours, I haven't seen anything encouraging except Rani's smile.

Her enthusiasm doesn't dim. My voice starts sounding so pitiful that no one stops to listen. I'm ready to give up for the day when Rani jumps up and drags me to my feet. "That's him. He's got your face!"

The man must feel our stare, because he glances back at us. I'm not sure what I expected, but this man's face, with its neatly trimmed beard and round glasses, is nothing like my reflection. "He can't be my grandfather. He's too young!"

"So what? Maybe he's your uncle. And see how scrawny he is? You have the same body type too. What more do you want?"

I want Amma more than anything else.

Also, I want Rani to be right. But I'm scared she's wrong.

Rani is the one who warned me not to hope too much. But now she's skipped over the hoping part and is acting totally sure that this stranger is my relative after one quick glance. She takes me by the arm and pulls me along. "Don't let him out of your sight."

I can't take my eyes off him anyway as we dodge through the crowd, a few steps behind him. I stare at the back of his head. Is it really shaped the same way as mine?

And maybe Appa does have a brother after all, and this man is my real uncle. A good, kind uncle.

*No. Out.* I try to fling away my hopeful thoughts. But though I can control my head pretty well, my heart hops about as if it wants to jump out of me and follow him on its own.

# 47

---

# Spying

We follow the man all the way to a tall concrete building. Off to the side of the building is an open staircase. The man climbs the stairs. I lose sight of him. "Now what?"

But Rani doesn't answer. Instead, she finds a tree behind the building and shinnies up as I watch from below, holding Jay's cage.

"Great! They live just one floor up," she reports. "Come on. You can get a great view from here."

Rani is so excited she tells me to hang Jay's cage on the tree, and then she helps me climb onto what she says are low branches, though it's higher than I've ever climbed before.

When I look down, I'm scared I'm going to fall flat on my

face. But when I look straight in through the open windows, I feel like I'm watching the end of a happy TV movie.

The man is sitting on a chair in front of a table full of food. A curly-haired toddler climbs into the man's lap and they laugh, while the woman watching them smiles. A boy sits with his back to me—but I'm sure he's smiling too. I've never seen a room so full of joy. This must be the kind of home Amma told me about.

"I hope he's your real uncle," Rani whispers.

It's scary to hear her say my wish out loud.

The spicy scent of the food wafts through the open window, right to my nose. My mouth goes watery, as if the food is mine.

Silly mouth. Hoping for food. Silly me. Hoping this happy family is somehow mine.

# 48

---

# Happy Family

I strain to catch snatches of conversation. When I realize the family is speaking in Tamil, my heart turns from a hopping frog into a heavy stone.

"They can't be my family! They aren't speaking in Kannada." I spit out the words.

"I—I'm so sorry. Maybe they speak both? After all, you and your mother speak Tamil and Kannada, right?" Rani pats my arm. "D'you want to get going?"

But I don't move because I can't stop watching this family. Now the father is trying to feed the toddler, who keeps turning away.

"Aha! Look, it's an airplane!" the father cries, making his

hand swoop around before bringing a spoonful toward the little girl. She giggles and opens her mouth wide.

"Very good," he says. "Can you open your mouth again, little crocodile?"

Would my father have been as patient as this little girl's? And would he have called me his little crocodile?

"You ready to go?" Rani tugs at my arm. "If someone spots us, they might think we're thieves and call the police to come beat us up."

But I can't leave yet, because the boy is telling his parents a story that upsets me. "A man climbed onto our school bus today. He had a huge stick . . . Threatened to crack open the heads of anyone from Chennai."

"What?" the mother cries out. "He threatened to beat up the Tamil children?"

"Yes . . . but the bus driver lied and said none of us were from there . . . He's a hero, isn't he, Amma?"

"Thank you, Allah, for looking after our children." The father's voice shakes.

The mother bows her head for a minute. Then she tells her son, "You are *not* going to school tomorrow."

"It'll be okay." The father raises his voice. "Tensions rise every summer. It always blows over. And our shop is in a safe part of town!"

"You are not going to work! The tensions are high *now*!" the mom shouts back, and the little girl starts crying. I look away. I don't like listening to the couple argue.

"You ready to go now, Kabir?"

I'm ready. I scramble down to the ground. I'm not family, and I don't belong here.

# 49

---

# Taking Charge

Rani picks a tree by a small lake, not too far from the building where the family lives, to be our new home.

She offers to fish for dinner—so we can save money. But she looks so tired, I offer to buy something with our remaining money instead.

I find a man with a pushcart who is selling roasted peanuts, and I get a good bargain—he gives me two large cones filled with freshly roasted peanuts wrapped in newspaper. If Grandma Knife was watching, I'm sure she'd be proud.

I put one of the nuts on my palm and offer it to Jay. He pecks at it cautiously, but Rani snatches it away, saying it's bad for him, and feeds him a handful of seeds from her shoulder bag.

"Sorry." I pop a handful into my mouth instead. Crunch. The peanuts fill my mouth with warmth. I chew them into a smooth paste. "This is the best thing I've ever tasted."

"Is that so?" Rani raises her eyebrows.

"Except for your cooking, I mean."

"It's okay." She grins. "I like peanuts better too."

I wonder what Amma's favorite snack is. All these years with her, I never thought to ask.

We save some peanuts for the morning, and then, with Rani's help, I climb the tree. It's scary, but clinging to branches and putting my foot where she tells me, I manage to get high enough to hide. Rani gives me a rope to tie myself to the branches.

"So let's talk to that man tomorrow," Rani says.

"Why?" I ask her. "He's not my uncle."

"Maybe he knows your grandparents. After all, they worship at the same mosque, right?"

"Or maybe . . ." Sad ideas start biting me like tiny ants. "Maybe they don't worship there anymore. Maybe—"

Rani turns to Jay. "D'you think Kabir *actually* threw hot coffee at his pretend uncle? Or was he lying about that?"

"I wasn't lying! I never lie!" I glare at her.

"Never! Never! Never!" Jay agrees.

"That's better!" Rani laughs, and I scratch Jay gently on the head to reward him for agreeing with me.

"Remember, Kabir—we chuck hot drinks or hard stones at life when it's trying to beat us down."

Rani's right. I have to be strong. In jail, Amma looked after me, and after that, Rani did. But here in Bengaluru, I need to prove I'm able to take charge.

# 50

---

# Hanging On to Hope

I try to hang on to hope, but it's the worst night ever, because I also feel like I have to hang on to the tree to keep from falling. I keep nodding off and then jerking awake with a start.

At last, tiny fingers of sunlight poke at my eyes. I wake Rani. "I'm ready to talk to the man. Let's go!"

"All right, all right," Rani murmurs sleepily.

Jay doesn't seem to mind rising early. He hops onto her shoulder jauntily when she lets him out of his cage.

Munching peanuts, we walk along the streets. Some buses are honking already, and a few cyclists are tinkling their bells, but the city isn't all woken up yet.

We stop in front of the building where the family lives, and before we can figure out how we're going to make our approach, the man comes hurrying out and quickly walks down the street.

"Looks like he's going to work instead of staying home like his wife wanted." Rani laughs softly. "Want to go talk to her?"

"No. Let's follow him instead. His wife might be in a bad mood after losing the argument."

The sky lightens as we follow him through a maze of streets, ending on one that's bordered with small shops. The man unlocks and rolls up a metal grate.

"Such a pretty headscarf!" Rani points at a bright pink scarf that flutters like a butterfly as the man hangs it up.

Thinking of my butterfly and pretending I'm holding it in my hands gives me courage. I ask Rani to wait for me at the corner, and I walk over to the shop.

"You're up early. What do you want, boy?" The man's voice isn't particularly kind. It's not at all the voice he used with his children yesterday.

But then, I'm not family. I'm not even a customer. I'm just

some kid off the street, the kind no one wants to look at, let alone speak to.

At least he said something to me. I want to say something back but can't seem to find my tongue, and all I manage is a sort of squeak.

"Came to buy your mother a sari?" The man grins as if he's made a joke.

"No, sir."

He starts polishing a counter.

"Sir, is your name Khan?" I ask.

"No, boy. Why?" The man narrows his eyes suspiciously.

I shift nervously from one foot to another. "My grandfather's name is Khan. I'm trying to find him and was wondering if maybe you knew him, sir, because he worships at the same mosque, I think?"

"How do you know where I worship? And what are you doing alone on the street so early?"

"Never mind." Tears prick at my eyes, and I try to hold them in, but they find their way out. Before the trickle can turn into a stream, I brush them off with the back of my hand.

I turn away, ready to race up the street to where Rani is waiting for me, but I see her racing toward us.

In the distance, we can hear the tramp of feet. Coming closer. And angry chants. Getting louder.

# 51

## Surrounded

The chanting dies off for a second, but then there's a loud crash. Triumphant whistles. A whoop before the chants resume—*"Tamils, get out!"*

"What're you waiting for?" Rani asks the man. "I can't understand exactly what they're saying, but I can tell that mob isn't singing the praises of Tamils. Lock up your shop, mister!"

At Rani's command, the man tears down the pink scarf that's hanging on the storefront. Rani and I take down another.

The man begins to yank down the metal grating in front of the shop. "Get in the shop, you two," he says, but Rani grabs Jay and plonks him onto my shoulder while she ducks out.

"Come back!" I shout.

"Can't breathe inside a box." Rani clambers up the water-spout on the side of shop and onto the low tin roof. "You stay and keep Jay safe."

"Help me up, mister! I need to stay with her!"

"Don't be silly!" the man says. But when he sees me struggling to get to Rani, he grunts, "Okay, then, but lie down and keep out of sight." He lifts me high enough that Rani can reach my hand and pull me up.

We lie on the tin roof and watch as five or six men turn the corner. I squirm like a rat caught in Grandma Knife's hands.

"This one is a Tamil store!" one of them shouts. "The owner is inside. I saw him!"

I lift my head slightly, just in time to see the tallest man aim a bottle at the storefront. I hear glass shattering and tinkling onto the pavement.

"Someone is on the roof," another man yells. "Bet they're Tamils too."

Rani pulls her slingshot and stones out of her waist pouch.

"No." I grab her hand. "You'll make them angrier."

"I'm not giving up without a fight," she whispers fiercely.

"Wait!" An idea strikes me, just like it did when I escaped from Fake Uncle. "You said other people are scared of the Roma and believe you can tell the future, so try this—stand up and repeat what I say in Kannada."

Rani pauses for a second, then leaps up and glares at the men as if she's their queen.

Jay cocks his head at her, and then at me, as if he's trying to make sense of what's happening.

Rani catches my Kannada words and repeats them without faltering. "Stop! You must leave now or you will suffer!"

For a moment, the crowd falls silent. Then a voice rasps, "That's just a kid up there!"

I prompt Rani and she continues, "Spirits of my ancestors— tell me, will these men get away with this destruction?"

Then I give Jay the cue to repeat my words, hoping he'll obey me as well as he obeys Rani.

"Never!" he echoes me. "Never! Never!"

"Did you hear that?" Someone in the crowd sounds scared. "It didn't sound human."

"Go'way, punk," Jay shrieks. And he adds the string of curse words he likes to attach to it.

"Let's leave now!" someone shouts.

But the tall man who threw the bottle is not to be stopped. He runs around the side of the building and starts clambering up the waterspout. "It's just two kids!"

"No!" I jump up and rush toward him. "No!"

He's trying to pull himself onto the roof, but I won't let him. I'll never let him lay a hand on Rani. I stomp on his fingers as hard as I can, again and again. He swears but doesn't let go and swipes at my ankles.

"No!" Jay's screech pierces my ear. "No, no, no . . ."

And then I hear another screech—the screech of a police siren.

Tires squeal. A police van pulls up and policemen pour out.

The bad men can't escape the police. They're trapped. But so are we.

# 52

Caught by the Police

We hear a thud and a howl—the sort of howl that came from the punishment block in jail. The police are down below, beating someone.

I crouch next to Rani and mumble a prayer. *God of the sky whom I can't see, please help me and Rani and Jay.*

Then someone's hands are on my shoulders. Steadying me. A strong—but also gentle—touch. I open my eyes.

It's a bearded policeman, on the roof with us. "You're safe now, children. Come on down." He helps me slither to the ground, and Rani follows.

"You need to come with me to the police station and answer

some questions, okay?" he says to Rani, who stares blankly at him.

"She doesn't speak Kannada," I say quietly.

"Glad you do. And I can speak Tamil too. Nice that you and I speak more than one language, isn't it? I'll use Tamil so you can both understand me." The policeman holds out his hand. "Trust me, little brother."

I feel dizzy. Rani and I climb into the waiting police van because they tell us to and there's nowhere else to go.

The store man gets inside our van too. He keeps saying, "Praise Allah we're safe."

I slide closer to Rani.

"May I take a picture?" he asks, his voice and hands shaking. "You two are heroes. You saved me. And my store. You bought us time so I could call the police. Can't believe how brave you were, distracting the crowd!"

I feel too tired to reply. But Rani looks worse, so I put an arm around her shoulders. Jay walks off my shoulder and onto hers.

The van stops, and we stumble out and into a police station. The store man is talking and talking, but my head feels as tiny as a butterfly's—too small to make sense of anything.

Another policeman takes the store man away, and our policeman takes us into a small room and asks us to sit down.

"Mr. Faisal says you two saved his life and saved his store. He says you warned him about the crowd, just in the nick of time. And then held them off until we came." The policeman tugs on his beard. "I believe him, and I'm sure you both are heroes, but I need you to tell us what happened too. Okay?"

"I hate indoors." Rani jiggles her legs. "I need to get outside."

"No one will hurt you here," the policeman promises. "Don't be scared."

"She's braver than me," I say quietly. "She just really doesn't like sitting inside rooms."

"How about we sit outside, then?" The policeman leads us to a yard, walled in and small, but open to the sky. "What do you like to drink?"

Rani squints at him, still suspicious, but says, "Soda."

"No problem. You too?" he asks me.

"Yes," I say, because I feel too tired to think. Or do anything more than link fingers with Rani. "Thank you, sir."

We sit on plastic chairs, and another man brings us drinks. My glass is tall. The outside is misty. When I touch it, it's wet. This time, I don't mind the fizzy bubbles scratching my throat. I feel lucky to be unharmed. I put my cheek against the cool glass. This police station is much nicer than the one where I met my uncle, and the policeman seems nicer too.

"Let's start with your names," the policeman says.

Rani presses her lips together in a tight line.

"We're here to help you," he says. "But we need you to speak to us."

I look into the man's eyes. Would Amma trust him?

The policeman strokes his beard and waits. Patiently. Silently.

I decide that the policeman's face and the touch of his hand— and just his way about him—are good enough to trust. He reminds me of Mr. Subramaniam, who helped us out at the ticket booth and said he used to be a policeman too.

My voice takes a little while to find. But when I do, I tell the policeman everything, because I hope telling the truth will help him trust me back.

Even though I was born behind bars.

# 53

---

# The Way Ahead

Rani's eyes flit over the wall that runs along the yard as if she wants to climb over it. "Can we go now?" she asks when I finish my story.

"I'd really like to help you," the policeman says. "Outside is not the safest place for kids on their own."

"But outside is where we live, sir," I say. "Us and lots of other kids."

"I just mean I want to help you both find a safe place to stay. No child should have to live on the streets."

"If you want to help, then can you help me find my grandparents, sir?" I ask.

"That's exactly what I want to try and do for you, Kabir. But in the meantime, you need a place to stay. I know a woman who runs a school—"

"Is it an orphanage? My mother didn't want me to go to an orphanage."

"No. Not at all. Look. Here's the school." He fishes a phone out of his pocket, types in a few words, and then shows me pictures as real as TV pictures, and even some short movies, showing kids talking and laughing.

The sound of their laughter makes Rani curious, I think, because I feel her breath on my shoulder as she peeks over me.

"It doesn't seem like a bad place to wait," Rani says, "while they're finding your family."

"Good. Now, how about some lunch?" The policeman leaves us with a policewoman, who sits with us in the courtyard when our food arrives and shows us some funny videos on her phone.

"Phones are like magic," I tell her.

"True." She laughs. "They call them *smartphones* for a

reason—you can find out pretty much anything you want to, using a phone."

"How does it know so much?"

"That's beyond me." She shrugs. "But here's how to find things on a phone. Look."

She shows me how to search famous people and places, step by step. It's fascinating to watch pictures of people and places pop up on the screen.

With her help, I can even look up all the people with the last name of Khan in Bengaluru. But it seems like there are thousands, so there's no way to know which ones might be my grandparents. But she says not to worry, the police are on it, and they've got other ways to search for people.

Afterward, our policeman returns, this time with a tall, skinny lady who is the head of the school he talked to us about.

Rani's feet twitch, and I'm scared she's still thinking of running away, but she surprises me by smiling back at the woman.

"Rani and Kabir?" Something about the woman's voice—firm but kind—reminds me of Bedi Ma'am. "I'm Viji Aunty."

I don't mind that she wants me to call her Aunty, even though she's no more my aunty than Aunty Cloud. And her Tamil is as good as ours, with the same accent.

"I'm told you've seen pictures of my Center for Children," she says. "We'd like to take you there. Do you have any questions for me?"

This must be the first time a grown-up has asked me if I had any questions. Not even Bedi Ma'am ever asked me that.

"If I come, can I leave whenever I want, if I want?" Rani asks. "And how do you punish kids who break your rules?"

"We don't believe in punishment," Viji Aunty says. "Our only rules are to be good to yourself and others. There's a wall around the school. But it's to protect against bad people coming in—to keep the children safe. If you ever wanted to leave, you'd just have to let us know, though we've never yet had a child who wanted to leave us."

"I'd have to sleep inside a room, wouldn't I?"

"Not if you don't want to," Viji Aunty says, and I see Rani's eyes light up for the first time since we arrived here.

Viji Aunty explains she has other children who live in tents on the property and have lessons under a banyan tree. "I'm never going to try and change the way anyone wants to live, so long as they're being good. But that said, I do want my students to get some schooling."

"Why?" Rani asks.

"So you have more ways to deal with the world out there."

"I can live without anyone's help," Rani says.

"I respect that," Viji Aunty says. "But learning things at school isn't going to take away your independence—it's going to add to it."

"Right," I chime in. "I like school, Aunty."

Viji Aunty flashes me a smile, then turns to Rani. "I'm sure you know, Rani, that your people came from India, but they now live all over the world. The Roma have traveled more than any other group of people I can think of. But they aren't respected as much as they should be. At our school, you could learn new things—and maybe someday, if you wanted, you could help Roma fight for equality."

Rani is quiet for a bit. I can almost see her thoughts floating away into the sky, imagining herself older.

"I think you'll be happy if you give it a chance, Rani," Viji Aunty says. "I've always believed there are many different roads you can take to get somewhere. And you look like a girl who can build a new road for herself if she needs it."

Viji Aunty asks the policeman if we can stay on a few hours, until the evening, so she can take care of a few errands. "And then I can pick you up later, if that's all right. You can try out the school for a few days and see if you like it."

"I guess it should be fine for them to stay here a while longer," the policeman says. "I've had a phone call—a lead I need to follow up on—so maybe you kids can get some rest out here in the courtyard."

He brings us a thick, beautiful cotton spread that's softer than any mat I've ever felt.

"Well, Prince of Mind Readers, you're pretty good at figuring out people," Rani says when we're alone. "Maybe even better than me. I'm glad you trusted this policeman."

She stretches out on the spread. I curl up next to her, stroke the thick cloth, and try to fall asleep, while Jay watches over us with his bright eyes.

# 54

---

# Time

When I wake up, it's dusk. Fireflies twinkle around me like a crowd of visiting stars. They're so pretty, I want to lie back and keep gazing at them, but I notice Rani isn't next to me.

I sit up and look around. No Rani anywhere.

Just a man and a woman, sitting on chairs, looking at me. The woman has a lined face that makes her look as if she's smiling even though she isn't. The man has a silvery beard, a crinkly forehead, and gentle eyes peeking out from beneath brows as straight as my own.

They watch me. I watch them back.

We're silent and still as statues. My body feels like it's floating in a dream, until a mosquito decides to bite me.

I slap the mosquito. At that sharp sound, the man's eyes snap as if he's waking up from a dream too.

The woman stretches out her arms. Her face gets so crinkled up, her eyes almost disappear.

"Kabir?" The man clears his throat a few times. "I'm your ajja, and this is your ajji."

My grandparents.

When I stay silent, my grandmother says, "Or you can say Thatha and Patti, if you prefer the Tamil words."

I have so many questions in my head that my tongue isn't sure which one to ask first. It doesn't move.

Which is fine, I realize, because Thatha and Patti aren't going anywhere. Apparently they've been waiting for me to wake up, sitting patiently while I slept.

After I escaped from Fake Uncle and Snake Man, a part of me has been running nonstop, and time has been running with me.

I no longer need to run.

# 55

---

# Trust

Our policeman strides into the courtyard. "I see you've met your grandparents, Kabir."

"How did you find them so quickly, sir?" It's easier for me to talk to our policeman, somehow. "And where's Rani?"

"Rani and Viji Ma'am are taking a walk together. As for finding your grandparents, that's the greatest success story of my career." He pats his beard proudly. "Mr. Faisal, the owner of the store, took photos of you and put them on the internet. He shouldn't have done it, but in this case, it helped. We have a good detective here—and with everyone on all sides working together, everything fell into place quickly. Apparently, your grandparents were on the lookout for you, and luckily they saw the photo Mr. Faisal posted."

"Amma said my father never told my grandparents about me." I turn to Patti and Thatha. "How could you have been searching for me?"

"The cook who works at the house where your father once worked contacted us some time ago," Thatha explains. "She said she'd seen you. She thought you looked familiar when she first saw you, then realized you reminded her of your father.

"She questioned that man, also named Khan, who claimed you were his nephew. She felt sure he was up to no good, and your disappearance strengthened her suspicions. She didn't trust the police, so she decided to try tracking down your father, and she found us."

Patti gets all choked up. "We are so grateful to her! It was so much to take in, after all these years, discovering we had a grandson, only to be told he was missing."

What a strange world. The chatty cook I met for a few minutes was kind enough to go out of her way to help me, but the policemen who'd worked in the jail where I'd lived all my life hadn't bothered to check if they were sending me to the right person.

And I'm so glad that this nice policeman did all he could to find my grandparents. "Thank you, sir," I say, and because it just doesn't sound like enough, I say it again a few times, as if I'm a parrot. "Thank you. Thank you. Thank you."

"It was nothing," he says, but he looks pleased as Thatha and Patti echo my gratitude.

"See this?" My Thatha holds out an old black-and-white photograph of a boy who could be me. His eyebrows are arrow-straight, same as mine. "That's your father when he was your age. We alerted the police in Chennai city. They're too busy to search for every poor child who goes missing, but it helped that we filed a report."

"I can't believe how much happened while I was sleeping," I say.

Our policeman smiles. "You've been sleeping soundly for quite a few hours, little brother."

My grandfather wipes his eyes. "We can go home, whenever you're ready," he says.

"Not yet," I say. "I'd like to wait till Rani's back, please."

My grandparents go indoors with our policeman while I wait

in the courtyard for Rani. In a few minutes, she returns from her walk, with Jay on her shoulder.

I rush over to her and blurt out, "I can't go to live with my grandparents unless you come too."

"What's this?" Rani puts her hands on her hips. "Now that we've found your grandparents, you don't want to live with them?"

"I want to be with you."

"Do you remember why you came to Bengaluru, Prince of Forgetfulness? You came to find your family."

"But I found you first. You're my best friend."

"I'm your only friend." Rani thumps me between my shoulders. "Seriously, Kabir, you're my best friend too, and I'll miss you—but I won't be that far away, you know?"

I blink really fast so that I won't cry. Finding Appa's family shouldn't mean I have to lose her.

"Kabir, listen. It's going to be okay. Remember how I told you my mother wanted me to go to school? Well, after I came to the city, I couldn't stand the thought of sitting in a room all day. Plus, I needed to figure out how to live on my own. But I've always felt guilty for not doing what my mother wanted. So I want to give Viji Aunty's school a try." Rani looks so hopeful, it makes me feel better.

"You promise we'll stay in touch?"

"Hmm . . ." Rani uses her fortune-teller voice. "Let me look into the future. Yes. Whether you like it or not, you are in my future. Isn't that right, Jay?"

"Right, right, rrrright!" Jay squawks.

I kiss the top of Jay's soft head. And I give Rani the longest hug.

When I let go, she gives me a little shove. "Don't worry," she says. "We'll both be fine."

I take a step and then another and then another.

I walk without looking back, all the way to where my grandparents are waiting.

# 56

---

# Finding My Father

Outside the police station, Thatha hails a rickshaw. We get in, and my grandparents squish me between them.

As the rickshaw putters along the road, darting through traffic, I drag to my lips the question that's been stuck in my heart for so long.

"Can you tell me what happened to my appa? Amma hasn't heard from him for years and years."

Tears wobble down my grandfather's cheeks. Patti swoops down and folds me in her arms. She smells like jasmine flowers—but I don't see any in her hair. Her arms feel softer than Amma's, but if I close my eyes, I can almost imagine Amma's holding me.

"Your father," Thatha says. "Sadly, your father died some years ago, Kabir. And all these years, we never knew he had a wife. Or a son. Not until the cook called us looking for your father."

Thatha's words sink in slowly.

Appa's dead. I'll never get to hold his hand or hear his voice. And we'll never be together, the three of us—Appa, Amma, and me—except for in my dreams.

Maybe Amma wondered if he'd died, and that's why she'd cry softly sometimes in our cell when she thought I wasn't awake. Maybe somewhere deep down, even I was afraid of it.

Thatha says something about how all this is so new while Patti dabs at the tears in her eyes. "We prayed for a miracle. We can't believe this is happening, but we're thankful it is."

"How did my appa die?"

"He died in a plane crash, Kabir," Patti says, looking at the ground. "He said he was coming home because he had something important to tell us. We used to wonder what it was. Now we know he wanted to tell us about the two of you."

"I'm afraid it's my fault my son was too scared to tell us the truth," Thatha says. "He was right to worry, because I had a fearful temper when I was younger. But sadness drove all the anger out of me after your father died." His eyes get shiny as if he's going to cry some more. "I never knew I had a grandson, but now all I know is I never want my grandson to be scared of me."

My father is dead. But maybe that's better than finding out he stopped caring about us. I wish I could talk to Amma right now and tell her she was correct—that he did always love us.

Thatha lays his large, warm hand on my knee. Patti squeezes me tighter, but my heart keeps sliding around in my chest as if it's a loose stone.

Because I miss Rani already. Because I'll never get to see Appa. And because if he isn't around to help me rescue Amma now, it's all up to me.

# 57

---

# Home

W elcome home." Thatha leads us to an apartment on the
second floor of a tall yellow building.

We take off our slippers outside the door, wipe our feet on a
thick mat, and step inside. My bare feet have never felt anything as smooth as the cool red-tiled floor.

The main room has a bookshelf with pictures of the boy who
was my father and the man he became.

"This is your father when he won a singing competition at
his school." Patti takes a picture down so I can see it up
close. My father holds up a funny-looking cup with two
handles. He wears a nice shirt and a pair of trousers and a
big smile.

"Here is more of your family." Patti starts pointing out faces and naming my father's cousins and their sisters and sisters-in-law and brothers and brothers-in-law. I see a lot of women who are really and truly my grand-aunties. And photographs of Patti and Thatha before their hair got gray.

"Want to see the rest of the house?" Patti says. "It's small, but I hope you like it."

Small? I wait for her to laugh, because it must be a joke.

She doesn't, although they—we—have not only this front room, but also two rooms big enough to fit two beds in them and a cupboard, plus a kitchen and a whole bathroom we don't need to share with anyone outside the family.

The bathroom hasn't got any grime anywhere. It smells funny in a way that tickles my nose, but not in a bad way.

"That's how clean smells," Patti says when she sees me take a deep breath.

The bathroom window is high up, but the bedrooms have large, low windows. I run my hands along the curly metal grille that's set inside the window frame.

"That grille helps help keep bad people out," Patti says. "Not that we ever had anyone break in. We look after each other in this neighborhood."

Patti's words remind me of what Rani said about Jay's cage. Gazing out the window at the narrow strip of sky above the neighboring apartment building, I wonder if Viji Aunty's school is as comfortable as Patti and Thatha's house.

"Want anything to drink? Or eat?" Patti says.

"No, Patti." I try out the word, and her smile grows as big as her face can fit.

"He can hardly keep his eyes open, poor boy," Thatha says. "Let him rest."

Patti gives me a bright white towel that smells lemony. And a tiny box with a soap inside that smells even nicer.

"For me? This whole new bar of soap?"

Thatha's lips wobble again, but Patti says yes, and she gives me a shiny new plastic comb and a toothbrush with a bright green handle. "That's for you too."

The toothbrush's bristles feel firm but not hard. The comb grins at me with all its teeth in place.

"Have you ever used a toothbrush and toothpaste before?" she asks.

"No, but I've seen it on TV. When I was with Rani, she showed me how to use neem twigs to keep our mouths clean, and in jail we rubbed a powder on our teeth."

Patti drops a tiny blob of paste onto my brush. The toothpaste fills my mouth with soft, sweet foam. I try swallowing some, and it doesn't taste as bad as seawater, but it definitely isn't good to eat.

The soap is orange and looks delicious. I'm tempted to nibble it, but Patti must be able to read my mind, because she says, "That's not tasty either, Kabir."

It's amazing how quickly the soap turns the water into a froth. Patti lets me play with the shiny soap bubbles in the sink for a while, but then she says I must stop because if I don't, my fingers will get as wrinkly as her skin.

# 58

###### ———

# Turning On a Light

In the room that Patti calls my bedroom, there's a calendar and a picture of something written in a long, beautiful script.

"That's Arabic," Patti says when she sees me staring at it. "It's the first verse from the holy Koran. You do know that it is our holy book?"

"Yes . . ." I remember Amma and Bedi Ma'am saying something about holy books. "But I—I don't know anything about it."

"Something tells me you'll learn fast." She smiles.

"Patti?" A worry that's been in my head finds its way out of my mouth. "Amma said Appa kept his marriage secret because Amma is Hindu. Are you upset I'm half Hindu?"

"Kabir, when I see you, all I think of is how great God is. You are a miracle we never dreamed about, never prayed for, never could imagine."

"But Appa should have told you about us!" I'm shocked by my own angry voice. It's like I bottled up my anger so long and so well I didn't even admit I felt it, but now it bubbles out like soda. "All these years we were in jail, we thought we had no one because of Appa being too scared to tell you the truth."

"Don't be angry with your father, Kabir. As your grandfather said, we were different back then." She pauses. "Losing your father changed us. No one can imagine the pain we felt. Our only child, gone."

"I understand pain," I whisper. My fists clench. "I bet *I* understand what pain means even more than you."

Patti takes my fists in her soft hands as sobs burst out of me.

"Go ahead, Kabir," she says. "Let it all out."

I grit my teeth, trying to hold back the anger and missing-Amma feeling and whatever-else feelings that slosh about inside my stomach like Rani's stew. But they gush up, and two rivers of tears start flowing down my cheeks.

They're pretty long rivers. They go on and on for a while. Patti slides her arm around my shoulders and waits until my tears stop. Then she gets me a cool glass of water. I take a sip and swirl the glass and listen to the ice cubes clinking together.

"We expected your father would marry a Muslim girl we chose for him," Patti tells me. "He kept putting it off, giving excuses, saying he wasn't ready for marriage, even though he was earning enough to help us move into this nice apartment. It was a shock to be told he already had a wife. A Hindu. And in jail. But then to hear he had a son! It was another shock for sure. But we agreed it was also a miracle."

Our fingers interlock. "So you don't mind I'm only half Muslim?"

She looks straight at me. "If your father had told us all those years ago he was marrying your mother, I'm sure we would have been angry. We probably would have acted badly toward him and your mother."

I'm glad she's telling me the truth. It would be so easy for her to lie. I'm glad she's not pretending.

"The fact that your mother chose a name for you that both Hindus and Muslims use means a lot to us. It's as if she sort of accepted us, even though we'd never met."

I look at the framed words hanging on the wall. I'm sure I'll enjoy learning new ways to pray to the God in the sky. After all, I'm good at learning songs by heart. "Patti, do you like Kabir's songs?"

"I don't know any because I hardly ever sing, which is probably a good thing, with my voice." She laughs. "But I like that Saint Kabir tried to bring Muslims and Hindus together. They say, after he died, his followers fought over whether to bury him or cremate him—"

"And then his body turned into flowers," I finish, happy there's at least one story that Patti and Amma share. "Then his Hindu followers burned half the flowers, and the Muslims buried the rest."

"Which shows they never did truly learn to come together," Patti adds softly.

"But I can, can't I? I want to learn both ways to pray. I want to bring both religions together inside me."

"Saint Kabir would be proud." Patti's cheeks crinkle into a smile. "So many gray hairs on my head, but I have a lot left to learn. I'll try my best."

"Patti, you'll help me get Amma out soon, won't you?"

"Let's talk about that tomorrow. Today was a lot for us, and I feel almost like I'm walking around in my sleep, scared this is just a dream." She gets up. "I can't imagine how tired *you* must feel. Shall I turn out the light?"

For the first time, someone is asking if I want the light on or off. No guards here to control my every move. If I want, I can get up anytime in the middle of the night for a drink of water or to go to the bathroom.

"Can I turn it off myself?" I ask.

"Of course," she says. "This is your home."

I press the switch and flick the light off, and then turn it on again. And off again. And on again.

*My light. My home.* I try on those words as if they're a new pair of slippers that don't quite fit.

But though I'm not yet used to this room, it already feels safe and so comfortable. I guess that's what Amma tried to tell me—home is a feeling, not a place. Except I won't ever feel truly at home until she's safe and comfortable with me.

"Thank you, Patti." I turn off the light.

"No need to thank us," she says.

The bed is just the right kind of soft. My pillow smells lemony, the same as my towel did. I lie back. It's nice the way my pillow holds my head up just a bit. I look out the window, my window, into the night sky.

Amma was right. Appa was a good man. He took care of his parents and he always loved us, even though he lived so far away.

I wonder if Appa is out there somewhere in the sky, near God, whether God's name is Allah or Krishna or something else I don't know, still loving us, still working to help Amma get out of jail in ways I can't see.

# 59

---

# A Little More Than We Need

Waking up in a real bed with a real pillow is so nice, I don't want to get out of it.

I lie in, watching a ray of sunshine turn bits of dust into gold, until I hear Patti enter the room, her sari swishing.

She puts a pair of shorts and a shirt on my bed that are warm to the touch. "Freshly ironed," she says.

She gives me a bottle of shampoo and tells me how to wash my hair with it. It's unbelievable how many things there are to help me stay clean. I like this shampoo, which makes my hair all foamy. I make a foam beard and try to look at myself in the bathroom mirror, but it's all misted up, and then the shampoo runs into my eyes and makes them sting.

By the time I'm ready to put on my new outfit, I feel not just clean but new. New Kabir, smartly dressed with shiny hair, ready to not just look at the outside world, but to try and belong in it.

Thatha says before breakfast, we should pray together, and he shows me how. Patti and Thatha pray very differently from anything Amma taught me. They also tell me they pray at least five times each day, which is a whole lot more praying than all the women in jail put together.

Patti sets a steaming cup of milk in front of me.

"I don't like milk," I start to say, but then I taste it, and it's nothing like the whitish water we got in jail. This milk is thick and creamy, and its taste sweetens my tongue.

"Changed your mind about milk? Now let's see how you like dosais." She plops dough onto a pan so hot it sizzles.

Soon, I'm munching on a hot, crisp dosai that's filled with fresh chutney made from ground-up coconut and coriander and chili, according to Patti.

"He's got a good appetite," Thatha says, looking up from the newspaper he's reading, as I eat dosai after dosai.

"You're the best cook ever!" I tell Patti.

After breakfast, Patti takes me shopping. Shopping is walking into shops and actually buying things they've got inside instead of just looking at them.

"My grandson needs some new outfits," she tells the store owner. He pulls a few shirts and some shorts off a shelf and tosses them onto a glass counter.

"So, Kabir," she asks me, "which do you like best?"

"They're all good." Not a single button missing or even loose.

"How nice, you're not a bit choosy." She buys me four new sets of clothes. And new slippers. She even gets me shoes, saying I have to get used to them before school starts. They look nice, but they make my feet feel trapped, probably like Rani feels when she's stuck indoors.

"Aren't you going to run out of money?" I ask. "I don't need so many clothes."

"This isn't that much," she says. "And sometimes it's nice to have a bit more than you need. Is there anything else you'd like?"

"I want Amma to be free," I reply. "Amma said my father was going to find a lawyer. Can't you and Thatha do that? Please?"

"I wish your mother were free too." Patti sighs. "But finding a lawyer to help when you don't have enough money to pay them isn't easy."

Patti sounds as if she's given up before she even started, and I'm not sure how to fight the hopelessness I hear in her voice.

"Now, anything else you want?" Patti says before I can respond. "Something that caught your eye?"

"A set of clothes for Rani," I say at last.

"Who?" Patti's forehead scrunches up.

"My friend," I reply.

"Oh! Yes, I remember her. But . . . I'm sure she has enough at that school where she's studying."

"Sometimes," I say, giving Patti her words back, "it's nice to have a bit more than you need."

Patti laughs, and then we buy a matching skirt and blouse for Rani.

Later, Patti teaches me how to use the phone to call Rani. We don't know the phone number, but with Patti's help, I search using the name of the school. It's strange hearing Rani's voice without seeing her, but it's still nice. Even though the first question she asks me is hard.

"How are you? Have you spoken to your dad yet?" she asks.

"No. He's . . . he's . . . dead."

"Oh, Kabir. I'm so sorry." For a few minutes, she says nothing, but it's comforting just knowing she's there for me at the other end. Finally, she speaks. "I guess it's one more thing we've got in common. You want to talk about it? Or something else?"

"Something else, please." I remember she never wanted to talk to me about her dad's death either.

"Okay, then. School? Are you at school yet?"

"No, because Thatha and Patti said the school where I'll go is closed for the summer, so I have some time off before I need to start." Time to get used to the outside a bit more, but I don't say that. "How are you?"

"Viji Aunty let me sleep in a tent outside, and there's a nice aunty who cooks the best food, and we can eat as much as we want, and one of the teachers gave me lessons under a banyan tree like the one in Chennai, except this one is bigger, and Jay loves it here too, and I made some friends already . . ."

She goes on and on nonstop. I love how happy and excited she sounds.

When I get off the phone, I look out the window and think of the God in the sky.

But I don't ask for anything. I just say, "Thank you."

# 60

---

# Free

When I wake up in the morning, I feel freer—and safer—than ever before.

I'm free to sing as loud as I want, anytime I want.

Free to open the windows of my room to let in the outside breeze. Or to turn on the ceiling fan that makes a breeze inside just for me.

Free when the afternoon sun gets hot to take a nap on my soft bed for as long as I please.

Free to add as many ice cubes as I wish to a tall glass of water and listen to them clink as I swirl the glass around before I sip and drink, sip and drink, thinking how lucky I am my throat will never again feel dry as a dead leaf.

I'm free. But.

Amma is still in jail. And a big piece of my heart is locked up there with her.

# 61

___

# Cousins

Amma and I can't talk on the phone, but we do write each other letters. Amma must be terribly sad to hear that Appa's dead, but she doesn't say anything about that and her replies are short—partly because she can't write too well— and she says she's happy I'm safe, and I should live my life and not worry about her.

As if I could.

I'm rereading one of Amma's replies to my letters when I hear a tapping on the front door.

"Can I open the door?" I jump up, and my grandparents laugh. It's fun to open doors from the inside—and decide if we want to let someone in.

Our visitors are a woman and a boy who's a lot taller than me. The woman greets my grandparents respectfully, and they welcome her and the boy in.

"This is Salma Aunty," Patti says to me. "She's your father's cousin who lives on the other side of the city. And this is her son, Junaid, who's just about your age. Isn't it nice to have a new friend, Kabir?"

"But I don't know him yet," I say, looking at the boy.

"Don't be rude," Thatha says sternly, though I didn't mean to be—all I was doing was telling the truth.

"You look exactly the same as your father when he was a little boy," the Salma woman says. "Junaid couldn't wait to meet you, Kabir."

"Why don't you boys go downstairs—fresh air is good for you." Patti shoos us out. "Just go play for a bit and come back up when you feel tired."

"Were you really born in jail?" Junaid asks as the door closes behind us.

"Yes."

"You're so skinny. Didn't they feed you?"

"Not too well."

"Did your mother rob someone?"

"No."

"Kill someone?"

"No!"

"What did they lock her up in jail for, then?"

"Nothing."

"I bet she did something really bad." Junaid sounds eager to hear a juicy story, and I'm tempted to kick him.

When I don't reply, he grunts. "Come on, Kabir, at least tell me what it was like in jail."

Even if I wanted to explain, I'm not sure I could. Jail was awful and stinky and scary in a different way than living outside. But in spite of how hard it was, I sometimes wish I were back there, because I miss Amma so much. And in jail, I had

Malli for a friend, who was so much younger but never asked questions as ignorant as Junaid's.

I'm guessing Patti might not like it if I told Junaid to shut up. So I stomp ahead of him, down the stairs, and out of our apartment building.

In the field between our building and the next, a group of boys are playing with a bat and a small ball. Cricket. I've seen it on TV, and I've seen them playing it before from the windows upstairs.

"I'm a great batsman." Junaid waves at them. "In fact, I'm so good that I might even play for India someday. Like Mohammad Azharuddin."

He goes on and on about himself. Hearing Junaid brag is a lot better than his begging me to feed him drama about my life. But it's still not much fun.

I decide I don't want to play a game I've never played before, with so many kids I don't know. Kids who will probably have sillier questions than Junaid's. I turn around and head back up the stairs as he runs off to join them.

"What's wrong?" Patti asks when I knock on the door.

"You told me to come back when I was tired," I remind her. "I'm tired of Junaid."

Junaid's mother sort of laughs. Thatha glares at me again.

"Feeling shy, maybe?" Patti asks. "Don't you want to make nice new friends?"

"Junaid wasn't nice," I reply. "He thinks Amma did something bad. And I already have nice friends. Outside I have Rani, and in jail I have Malli."

"Rani?" Thatha has forgotten her, just like Patti couldn't remember who she was when we went shopping.

"The Roma girl," Patti says.

"She's got a name!" I shout, because I know it's rude, and Patti and Thatha think I'm rude anyway. "Rani is my friend! She looked after me!"

I run into my room and slam the door and lock it from the inside and lie on my bed.

Laughter floats in through the window—maybe Junaid is out there telling the cricket boys something funny about me.

# 62

## Not Perfect

Outside my room, I hear Patti and Thatha speaking in low voices. Probably discussing how to punish me. I wonder if they'll hit me with a ruler. Mean Teacher liked to do that.

A soft knock sounds on my door.

"Kabir, please let us in." Patti doesn't sound angry. Just sad.

I feel a little bit bad that I upset her after all she's done for me. I open the door partway.

"We're sorry," Patti says.

She sounds truly unhappy. The monsoon storm of rage that

just burst out of me starts to weaken. I let the door swing all the way open.

"We know your friend—Rani—means a lot to you, and it was wrong of us to . . . to—to think of her as anything other than your friend," Thatha mumbles.

They come in and sit on my bed with a space between them. A me-sized space.

"When I set eyes on you—no, even before that," Patti says. "All those days we feared you were lost on the streets of Chennai, I promised myself that if we ever found you, I'd be the perfect grandmother. But I guess I'll be making a lot of mistakes."

"It's a long time since we had a little boy." Thatha rubs the worry lines cutting deep into his forehead. "We've forgotten a lot."

"I'm not little," I say, but I go to sit between them.

"You're still young, Kabir," Thatha says. "You're a hero too. So brave. But you never had a chance to be a child until now."

"Of course I've had a chance to be a child," I tell him. "I'm doing it right now."

Patti smiles, and then asks, "What happened with Junaid?"

"Junaid acted as if Amma was a terrible criminal. Like she killed someone." I spit out the words. "But she never did anything wrong. Not a single thing."

"Right," Patti says.

"Sure," Thatha agrees.

I peer at them, trying to tell if they're lying for my sake or if they truly mean it.

"Trust us. Please," Patti says. "We're sure your mother is wonderful, Kabir, because of how wonderful you are. She raised you without any help, in jail, and look at you. Kind and thoughtful and polite."

"Polite most of the time, anyway." Thatha chuckles.

"If you believe Amma is innocent, why won't you find a way to get her out?" I ask.

"We would, if only we had more money." Thatha's smile falls away. "Lawyers are so expensive. But we can start saving . . ." He sounds defeated already.

Saving would probably take forever, and I'm tired of waiting. Amma should never have been in jail, and she shouldn't have to wait another minute. I need to make a plan.

Patti is still talking about Junaid. "I'll speak with his mother," she says. "I'm sure Junaid won't act that way again, once she gives him a talking-to. Give him a chance, Kabir; he's your cousin, after all. Maybe you'll be friends one day. He just doesn't know any better right now, poor fellow."

Friends? With Junaid? I have a good imagination, but even I can't imagine that.

Plus, there's nothing poor about him. I'm the one who was in jail all my life.

# 63

---

# At the Bazaar

Want to come to the market?" Patti asks after breakfast next morning. "You can choose what you want me to make for dinner tonight."

The bazaar is the best place we've gone so far—a narrow street with fruits and vegetables and all sorts of other food stalls on either side. Vendors shouting in singsong voices to attract passersby, just the way Rani and I used to do.

Everyone at the market greets Patti as if she's their own grandmother. She stops and talks and buys potatoes and carrots from a young woman who sits behind hills of vegetables. Then we walk over to a young man who has sacks filled with rice and all sorts of uncooked grains. Patti sifts bright orange lentils with her fingers before she buys some. Patti explains how a balance works while I watch the man pack the lentils for us.

When Patti sees me eye a fruit that's bottle-green and bigger than my head, she says, "Haven't you ever tasted watermelon?"

We walk right over, and the watermelon seller teaches me how to test if a watermelon's ripe. "You knock on it and flick its skin. Hear how this one sounds hollow, but this doesn't?"

I can't tell the difference, but it doesn't matter, because he chooses one.

"This," he says, smacking his lips, "will taste so mmmm . . . good."

"How much?" Patti asks.

"Free for you this time." The watermelon seller ruffles my hair. "Nice to see your grandson visiting you after all these years."

"He lives with us now," Patti says. "Such a handsome, smart, polite boy—though we can't take any credit for that. His mother raised him right."

I smile all the way back to our apartment building. When we near it, I see some boys playing cricket.

"Your father was a very good batsman, you know. You want to play with them?" Patti suggests.

"Maybe another time. I need to help you carry the groceries now. And maybe I can help you cook?"

"Your father loved to help me cook too," Patti tells me. "Not a lot of boys helped their mothers in the kitchen, but he always did things he enjoyed and didn't worry about what others thought. He was never scared to try new things either—like moving to Chennai on his own, and then to Dubai. He used to say, 'Fear is a lock, and courage is a key we hold in our hands.'"

When I hear Patti speak about my father, it's as if she's digging a big hole in my heart, but also filling up a hole in my mind.

It sort of hurts, but still, I love learning about him. And I want to know all I can, because it brings me as close to him as I'll ever get.

# 64

---

# Locks and Keys

After I help her make lunch, and we're all full, Thatha heads off for a nap. Before Patti joins him, she asks, "Would you like to use my phone? You could call your friend again. Or find a game to play or something to watch or read, maybe?"

"Oh, yes, thanks." I do want to search for something, though not a game or a book. And I have an idea. As soon as she disappears into her room, I punch the words *lawyer* and *Bengaluru* into the phone.

A few more minutes of work, and I find a long list with names, addresses, and phone numbers. I get a pencil and paper and copy a few phone numbers so I can get started.

Patti's whistling snore joins Thatha's low rumble. I walk onto the balcony, as far away from Patti and Thatha's room as I can get, and call the first number.

My voice is my strength. It doesn't tremble. My fingers do. I'm glad the person at the other end can't see me.

"Good afternoon," I say in my politest voice. "I'm looking for a good lawyer."

"Yes?" The person sounds annoyed already.

"My mother's in jail for a crime she didn't commit—"

The person hangs up. So what? There are lots of lawyers on my list!

I cross off the first number and try the second. And I don't get very far. But I think of what Patti told me my dad used to say—*Fear is a lock. Courage is a key.*

On the third try, I do get a bit further. The man at the other end listens to my whole story, wishes me good luck finding a lawyer for free, and hangs up. I can't tell if he's being mean.

Then I hear Patti and Thatha waking up, so I stop and look at the boys playing cricket down below. Yelling and running and standing still, watching the ball speed toward the batsman as if nothing's more important.

That night, before Patti lets me turn off the light, she says, "I saw the calls you made, Kabir."

I didn't know she could. But it's not as if I did something wrong. So I don't say sorry.

"You look so small for your age." She pats my head. "But you're so brave not to give up on trying to help your mother."

Patti's words are sweeter than golden laddus and airy soan papdi. Hearing her now makes me realize I'm starting to love my grandmother for real. Not just because I'm supposed to.

"Can I keep trying?" I ask. "There are so many lawyers in this city, Patti. I'm sure someone will help."

"Fine. But I don't want you getting your hopes up," she warns. "And I don't want you sitting indoors all day getting disappointed. I'll let you use my phone for a little while each day if you promise me you'll go out and play with the boys."

"I promise."

After Patti leaves, I stare out the window at the moon. It's torn in half, but I remember what Rani said.

It'll grow back.

# 65

---

# Truth and True Friends

The next day, as we return home from the market and pass the boys playing cricket, a ball comes flying at us. I reach up and catch it.

"Howzaatt!" the boys cheer. "He caught it—you're out."

"No way!" the boy holding the bat complains. "He's not on your team!"

"He is now!" a boy wearing spectacles shouts, and looks at me. "You wanted to play with us, right?"

"Go on," Patti says. "We didn't buy much today. I can carry the bags upstairs."

"Come on!" the spectacled boy says. "Join us!"

Patti is marching up the stairs already. I promised her I'd play with them. I stay.

The spectacled boy runs over. "Good catch! When did you move here? Are you going to join our school when it reopens? How old are you? I'm Lakshman. What's your name?"

I'm glad he asked so many questions, because I can choose which one to answer. "I'm Kabir."

"Are you as good at batting as you are at fielding?"

"I'm not sure—I don't know much about cricket, actually," I confess.

"How come you don't know anything about cricket? Did you come from some foreign place where you played some other sport?"

"Sort of. Can you explain cricket's rules? I've watched you play from our apartment. It looks pretty complicated, but I learn fast."

"Sure. Tomorrow, come over to my place in the morning and I'll explain all the rules. But you don't need to know them to play. For now, you can be a fielder. That's easy—you just run

after the ball and catch it and throw it to one of your teammates. Come on." He waves to the other boys.

The other boys run over and crowd around me, saying what
a good catch I made. The batsman looks a bit grumpy, but
even he says hello.

I'm nervous and make a couple of mistakes, but I also pull
off two more "spectacular catches," according to Lakshman,
so my teammates are pretty happy with me. When we're
done, I feel a nice kind of tired. The boys break up and
walk to different buildings, except for Lakshman, who
joins me.

As we walk up the stairs of our building together, he chatters away. "Cricket is a great way to make friends. Trust me.
I didn't know anyone when we moved here from Chennai
last year. Where did you move from? Or are you just visiting? I've seen you with your grandmother. Where do your
parents live?"

I hesitate, but only for a minute. Telling him the truth will be
a test that'll show me if he can be as nice a friend as Rani. If
not, I don't want to make friends with him.

"My father's dead."

"I'm sorry. That must be so hard," he says. "My grandfather died last year, and I still miss him. Where's your mother?"

"The police put my mother in jail, even though she didn't do anything wrong," I say. "I'm trying to find a lawyer to get her out."

"Oh!" Lakshman looks impressed. "You are? How's that going?"

"I've not had much luck yet. But I'm not giving up. There must be some generous lawyers, right?"

"Of course. There's all sorts of good people in the world." Lakshman's smile is so bright, my heart feels lighter. "When I grow up," Lakshman says in a grand voice, "I am going to become a lawyer who helps people who don't have money. You think I can do that?"

"Why not?" I smile, thinking of Bedi Ma'am's words, which feel so long ago now.

"You want to become a lawyer too?" he says. "We could fight for justice together."

"Sure," I say, although I've never thought about it before.

"Or maybe a policeman. You know, a good policeman, like in movies."

"Okay," I say, but Lakshman changes his mind again.

"Or maybe we could make movies that are so good that everyone who watches them will want to change the world. Or else—"

"Okay, okay." I laugh. "You have a lot of good ideas. How about we decide later?"

"All right. And thanks!" Lakshman looks really pleased with himself at my compliment. "So is anyone else helping you, or are you working all on your own?"

"I was all on my own, but . . ." Lakshman's question is like a switch turning on a light inside my head. "There is someone who could maybe help. She's the head of my friend's school."

"Everyone in my school is terrified of our headmistress. No one I know would ever ask a headmistress for help with anything."

"This one isn't scary at all. She even lets my friend Rani sleep outdoors and have lessons under the trees."

"Lessons under trees?" Lakshman echoes. "I want to go to that school!"

"Anyway, I could call her . . ."

"Wait, want to go there instead? I want to see this school." Lakshman's eyes sparkle behind his glasses. "We can go tomorrow, just us two. It'll be our first mission for justice."

"Okay, fine." I'm glad I finally have a plan. And it'll be fun to see Rani and Jay again. "Let's do it."

# 66

---

# A School with a Tent

At dawn, I leave a note on my bed for my grandparents and sneak out of the apartment while they're still snoring away like a couple of elephants.

> *Patti and Thatha,*
> *Please don't worry. Lakshman and I have gone to visit*
> *Rani, and we'll be back later today.*

As planned, Lakshman is waiting for me downstairs. He knows all about buses, and we buy tickets with the bit of leftover money from Earring Aunty. He chatters nonstop, and it feels like no time till we reach Viji Aunty's Center for Children.

The school is a walled compound as big as a jail, but with an inviting gate and a friendly watchman who waves us in as soon as I say I want to see Viji Aunty. Pretty creepers with pink and white flowers that Lakshman calls bougainvillea hang over the wall.

Scattered on the grounds are clusters of small houses with sloped roofs. "I wonder where Rani is. Do you see a tent?"

Just then, a familiar screech suddenly pierces my ears. "Ai! Ai! Ai!"

"What's that?" Lakshman looks startled.

"Kabir!" Rani runs up behind us. "You never said you'd be visiting, Prince of Surprises!" She throws her arms around me, and Jay reaches out his beak and nips my ear excitedly.

"I've missed you both." I hug Rani back. "I brought you something. Look." I give Rani the gift bag with the outfit from Patti.

She takes it but turns her attention to Lakshman. "And who are you?"

"I'm Lakshman, Kabir's new friend. I came from Chennai too, you know. Kabir said you get to sleep in a tent and have lessons under trees. Can we see?"

"I'll show you both around. Come on. Oh, and this is Jay," Rani tells him.

"What a pretty bird," Lakshman says.

"Pretty, pretty, pretty bird," Jay squawks, making us all chuckle.

As we walk to Rani's tent, other children wave and greet her. I'm not surprised she has a million friends here already.

Rani's tent is bright green and sits under the shade of a tamarind tree. A few other tents are spread out on the grass behind hers. She tells us they are made from thick pieces of canvas tied onto poles, and they are large and airy inside.

Lakshman walks around Rani's tent, examining it from every side, and the two of them chat happily about what it's like to live in one. "This is the best tent I ever saw." He sighs happily. "You're so lucky!"

Rani still has her slingshot and shoots some fruit down for us. "Luckily I don't have to hunt crows for breakfast anymore," she says to me.

"Crows?" Lakshman looks curious. "How do they taste?"

"Hope you never find out," I mutter. "But squirrels taste worse." I feel a bit left out by the way he's chattering with Rani, but only a very little bit. It's nice to see how well they get along.

"I'm sure I'd do much better on my tests if I could learn outdoors," Lakshman says as we stroll along, past a shady banyan tree, beneath which a teacher sits on a straw mat with a group of children surrounding her.

"Indoors has *some* advantages, though," Rani says. "I'm getting better about spending time indoors, Kabir, can you believe it? When the rains start, I'm thinking I might be more comfortable inside."

"What? You'll be living under a roof?" I can't believe my ears. "You must be really happy here, Rani."

"It's nicer than I thought it could be," Rani says. "Viji Aunty encourages independence. She wants to help me grow." Rani sounds chirpier than I've ever heard before. "How are you doing, Kabir? Are your grandparents good? Where are they, anyway? Didn't they come with you?"

"No," Lakshman says proudly. "We came on our own. We're on a not-so-secret mission."

"My grandparents are really nice. But I can't stop thinking about Amma." I extend a hand, and Jay hops onto it. "They don't have money to hire a lawyer, so I need to do something—that's our mission. I thought maybe Viji Aunty could give me advice. Would that be all right?"

As if on cue, Jay lets out a piercing "Right, right, riiight!"

"Ai! Softer, Jay!" Rani grins. "Come on. Let's go find Viji Aunty. She loves helping."

# 67

---

# Up and Down

Viji Aunty seems very relieved to see me. "Your grand-parents called to see if you're okay, Kabir. Apparently you gave them quite a fright, running off on your own so early. Next time you visit, bring them with you, all right?"

She calls them, and we have a quick chat. She makes Lakshman call his parents. And then, at last, I explain to Viji Aunty why I'm here and how I want to help Amma.

Viji Aunty listens carefully and patiently, and when I'm done, she says, "My brother's wife works for a law firm that helps people who can't pay, Kabir. Her name is Tanvi. I'll give her a call."

Viji Aunty is able to reach Tanvi Ma'am right away, and after chatting with her for a bit, she puts me on the line.

After I fill her in, Tanvi Ma'am says in a voice as brisk as a jail guard's, "Your mother has been in jail far too long. Even for aggravated theft, the punishment is seven years. I can't promise, but I think this is a straightforward case. I'll be happy to work on getting her released."

"So you can prove Amma is innocent?" My heart soars. At last, the truth will come out.

"Hold on, Kabir. At this point we don't need to prove anything. Your mother has already spent more time in jail than if she'd been convicted."

"But I want everyone to know she is innocent."

"I can't prove what did or didn't happen nearly a decade ago," Tanvi Ma'am says. "I'm truly sorry. But the main thing is, you want her out as soon as possible, don't you?"

Of course I do. "Yes! Thank you," I whisper, because though I don't feel like shouting with joy anymore, I am grateful. "Thank you, ma'am."

My heart feels as if it's a cricket ball, rising up one minute only to head straight to the ground a minute later.

"What did she say?" Rani asks as soon as I hang up.

When I explain that Tanvi Ma'am promised to help Amma leave jail because she has been there too long, both Rani and Lakshman cheer. Jay screeches, but Viji Aunty just beams at us all.

But when I add that even Tanvi Ma'am can't prove Amma is innocent, Lakshman bursts out, "That's so unfair! When we grow up, we'll prove she didn't do anything wrong, okay?"

His words make me smile.

"Aunty, I—I—" I'm not sure how to tell Viji Aunty how grateful I feel.

Viji Aunty waves away my thanks. "I once lived on the streets," she says.

"You did?" Lakshman clearly wants to hear more too, like me.

Viji Aunty says, "Let's save my story for another day."

We say our goodbyes, and Rani walks us to the gate. On the ride home, I focus only on the good news, and my heart feels lighter. Amma will be coming home soon.

I don't feel like I'm on a bus. I feel like I'm on a plane.

# 68

---

# Routines

Every afternoon, I walk to the market with Patti, and after I help her carry our groceries upstairs, Lakshman knocks on our apartment door and we run downstairs to play cricket. The boys downstairs aren't all as nice as Lakshman, but they're not all nasty Junaids either.

From the upstairs window, Thatha watches us playing. When it gets too dark to see the ball properly and mosquitoes start munching on us, Patti's voice floats down—"Time for dinner, Kabir!"—and I walk back up the stairs, following the delicious scent of her cooking.

Best of all, once a week, Tanvi Ma'am calls to chat with me about my mother's case. Each time we talk, she sounds more cheerful. One day, she tells me people are looking into the conditions at our jail. "The superintendent was fired," she tells me, "and we will be working to free more women and to make sure life will be better for those who remain in jail."

Life in there couldn't get much worse.

I think of the skinny tree in the jail schoolyard and how much it must have struggled to grow without anyone taking care of it. I suppose Amma is struggling in her own way, scared to hope that I'll actually be able to get her out of jail, because it's hard enough just to get through each long jail day.

In jail, every day had the same routine.

After jail, with Rani, days were never the same, because nearly everything felt new.

I felt scared a lot, though, which feels kind of like jail too. I'm learning to break out of the fear now, taking small steps each day.

Patti and Thatha help, bringing me new things to see, hear, taste, touch, and smell every day, so I'm busy trying to match real things up with the pictures my head kept inside it or made up from books and TV.

But we eat meals in the same room at the same time each day. And we pray the same way at the same times, waking to the sound of the call for prayer floating in from the nearby mosque. I'm not yet ready to visit the mosque, though Thatha keeps saying he wants to show off his grandson—but soon, I'm sure I'll feel brave enough to meet his friends and our extended family and even my cousin Junaid again.

For now, I'm enjoying learning new routines. At Patti and Thatha's home, repetition feels comforting, like a song's rhythm.

# 69

---

# The Shape of the Sky

Cricket comes easily to me, as if Appa handed his skill down to me somehow. One evening, I play the best shot a batsman can ever make. I whack the ball so hard it flies up over the boundary, and I score six runs with just that one shot.

My teammates and I jump up and down.

"Super!" a deep voice shouts. It's Thatha, standing there watching us! He usually just peers down from an upstairs window.

He looks happy—but he has never interrupted us before. "Thatha?"

"Sorry, boys, but I need to steal my grandson from you now,"

Thatha says. He smiles at me, but his tone is serious. "Kabir, come on home. I have something to tell you."

Upstairs, Patti joins us. We sit around the creaky table, and Thatha says, "Ready to pack your suitcase, Kabir? We're going to Chennai tomorrow, and we're going to bring your mother—our daughter-in-law—back home."

My heart starts racing around inside my chest, even though I'm just sitting on a chair, not running, not walking, not doing anything except smiling.

Outside the window, clouds puff out, changing shape. Every shape they take looks perfect, and the size of the sky outside the window feels perfect too.

I don't think I can feel any happier, but I do when I call Rani to give her the good news.

"I knew you'd do it!" She whoops. "But I never thought it would happen so fast. This is a miracle!"

"I didn't do anything. Viji Aunty's lawyer friend is the one who made this miracle happen."

"There'd be no lawyer if you hadn't come here to find your father's family," she reminds me.

"I wouldn't be here if you hadn't found me," I remind her.

"Did you hear that, Jay?" I hear the smile in her voice. "We helped save Kabir's mother. Are you proud?"

Jay shrieks something I can't make out, but he sounds just as happy as she does.

# 70

―

# Back Behind Bars

Tanvi Ma'am meets us the next day to take us back to jail. She's pretty, with pointy glasses and a pointy chin and a black braid that reaches down to her waist.

We get into Tanvi Ma'am's car. It has smooth seats and music and air-conditioning—which is an amazing way to make the inside cool, though it's hot outside. As Tanvi Ma'am's driver speeds along the roads, my heart is singing, which I never knew it could do, repeating words like Jay does: *They're going to let Amma out, let Amma out, let Amma out!*

When we arrive outside the spiky gates, I realize I'm actually chanting the words out loud. A guard unlocks the gates to let the car drive in, and in the rearview mirror I see the guard lock the gates behind us again.

Then I'm back inside.

Uniformed men take my grandparents' phones and even their keys, and we walk through something that Tanvi Ma'am says is an instrument made to detect metal. They pat us down too, looking for weapons. I don't mind, because they're almost polite, saying "good afternoon" and "sir" and "ma'am" to Thatha and Patti and Tanvi Ma'am, and even once jokingly saluting me.

We walk in through doors unlocked before us and locked again behind us.

Clanging metal and squeaking keys make me feel jumpy. Thatha must sense this, because his hand squeezes mine just a little tighter.

Tanvi Ma'am talks to a bunch of policemen, and their voices blur like ocean waves, because all I want to hear is Amma's soft voice again. Everything fades except the thump of my heart as we sit in cold metal chairs and wait.

And then, there she is, Amma, wearing the widest smile I've ever seen; there she is, with Grandma Knife right behind her, saying in her rusty voice, "I thought I heard you promise your amma that once you left, you'd never return to jail?"

My movements are jerky as I stand up. I'm too confused to reply, but then Amma chimes in, "Some promises should be broken."

Suddenly I'm caught inside the circle of Amma's arms. I'm shouting, "Amma, Amma, Amma!" and no one tells me to stop.

Amma starts bawling, and I do too. I don't know why, though, because it's the best moment of my life.

But then I hiccup, and she starts hiccuping with laughter, and we're laughing when we break off our hug, though we're still holding hands.

"Well, I must say," Grandma Knife cuts in, "I'm pretty impressed you managed to get your mother out so fast."

"Your tips helped me out of some really tough spots," I tell her. "Especially the one about chucking stuff at people you can't trust."

"Ai," she says. "That's a good one."

I laugh. "How are Aunty Cloud and Mouse Girl?"

Amma looks confused, but Grandma Knife catches on right away.

"Aunty who and who? Don't explain, boy, I know just what you mean." Grandma Knife laughs so hard, tears wriggle down her cheeks. "What secret nickname did you give me?"

"Grandma Knife," I admit. Amma gasps, but my real grandparents find this as funny as Grandma Knife does.

"All this while I thought you were such a sweet boy." Grandma Knife wipes her eyes. "Aunty Cloud, as you call her, got her day in court, and they let her out. She's living with her eldest son—I just heard from her. As for Mouse Girl, I'm doing my best to keep her from turning into a Rat Girl, poor thing."

"Grandma Knife," I say, "when I grow up, I'm going to become a lawyer and help you get out too, okay?"

"Never mind me, boy." Grandma Knife gets all serious. "All I need to keep going is the sight of you two leaving together."

"Well, here's something else to keep you going—some fruit for you, and sweets for my friend Malli." I give Grandma Knife two packages. "Can you get it to her?"

"Of course."

Knowing Grandma Knife is going back to her cell saddens

me, even though she acts as if it's fine. I know the world isn't perfect—inside jail and outside it. But I thought this day would be.

"Don't you be upset, Kabir." Grandma Knife waves jauntily as if she's the one leaving jail. "In here, with a roof over my head and food in my stomach, is a good place for my body to stay, knowing you two are out there praying for my soul—if I actually have one."

After Grandma Knife leaves, Thatha and Patti introduce themselves to Amma.

Amma presses her hands together and bows. She stammers her thanks to them.

Amma and Patti and Thatha are smiling nervously at one another and standing sort of together but also sort of awkwardly apart. And I know what's missing: me. I'm like a missing puzzle piece they need, the piece that will make everything else fall into place.

My chest feels tight, as if my heart has suddenly grown huge. I stare at the three of them.

My family. My family is together, though not exactly the way I'd imagined it.

I feel a pinch of sadness in my heart because my father isn't with us. But my world is also a whole lot bigger than I could have ever imagined, because now it holds Rani and Jay and Lakshman and my grandparents inside. So much good that I didn't even know about.

Best of all, Amma is free—free to turn her back on this building forever, free to live outside with me.

"Ready to go home?" Tanvi Ma'am asks, and she leads the way out.

As my family steps into the dazzling sunshine, I start to sing the happiest song I can think of.

Amma joins me. Her voice is trembly, so I say, "I'm here. Don't worry."

"I'm not," she says. "I'm not worried at all."

We hold hands and start singing again. Our voices are stronger than ever—and together they climb right up into the wide-open sky.

# Author's Note

This novel is inspired in part by a BBC news report I read nearly a decade ago, in 2013 (www.bbc.com/news/av /world-asia-22677788). These facts embedded themselves in my mind: A boy had been born in jail, and when he was set free, he fought to free his mother, who had languished in jail without a trial because she was too poor to post bail. The seeds of two characters had been planted, and they grew into their own, bringing with them a story whose roots reached into the story of my friend Indira, from the Roma community. The details about the Roma community provided in this novel are based on information Indira shared with me and my mother, who volunteered to help at the Kuravar Patashalai (School for Roma Children) in Chennai when I was a child. I also read books and articles on the Roma community of India.

In addition, I read books and articles on jails in India, visited a prison, and spoke to people who worked with inmates. I named Kabir's teacher Bedi Ma'am in honor of Kiran Bedi, a social activist who greatly improved the conditions of prisoners in Tihar Jail in India. In the United States, there are many organizations working to help those who are incarcerated or who have an incarcerated relative, such as Poetic Justice (poeticjustice.org) and CLiF (clifonline.org/literacy-programs/children-of-prison-inmates), which undertake projects that involve books and reading. The Innocence Project (innocenceproject.org) seeks to overturn wrongful convictions, and the Equal Justice Initiative (eji.org) works hard for children's rights and to keep children from being imprisoned, because this is another shocking human rights abuse that occurs in our nation and across the world.

Unfortunately, inequities and injustices continue to be perpetrated against incarcerated people in our nation and across the world. For instance, arrested people can be sent to jail, but they're supposed to be tried in court soon after. Only criminals who are proven guilty are supposed to serve long sentences in prison. In India, as in the case of Kabir's amma in the novel, people who belong to socioeconomically oppressed groups are far more likely to suffer police brutality and may even end up serving more time in jail as "undertrials" (those who are being held although they have never had a chance to argue their cases in court) than if they were prosecuted for the crimes for which they are accused. In India, police distrust is common among people considered to be "low-caste" because of corruption, cruelty, and police brutality against low-income and low-caste people. In the United States, people who are Black are far more likely to be subjected to police brutality and also to be wrongfully convicted. I first learned about anti-Black prejudice in our criminal justice system while analyzing statistics in a categorical data analysis class taught by Professor Bob Diaz decades ago, but unfortunately this terrible injustice continues today.

Water is one of our most precious resources, and regardless of where we live, we should take steps to conserve it (epa.gov /watersense/watersense-kids). Due to climate change crises, water scarcity is increasingly common in the United States and elsewhere. In India, droughts have been more severe in the recent past, and people in the crowded city of Chennai frequently face water shortages. Disputes arise, tension builds, and sometimes, violence erupts (cnn.com/2016/09/13/asia /india-water-dispute).

I've seen and experienced hatred and prejudice firsthand in each of the five countries where I've lived. But I've also rejoiced in love and friendship in each of these countries. I hope Kabir's story will engender compassion and empathy, raise important questions about how we might choose to act peacefully to change ourselves and our society, and help to shape a better future for our world, no matter where we live.

# Acknowledgments

My career as a writer would not be the same without certain people. First and foremost, my editor, Nancy Paulsen, and my agent, Rob Weisbach. Nancy is brilliant and insightful. I'm immensely fortunate to have a legendary editor who believes in me and my work. Rob sees my first drafts when they're as amorphous as amoebae, and yet never refuses to read anything I send him. He's always ready to make me laugh and always willing to listen. And my speaking agency, The Author Village, is amazing.

I've long admired Pernille Ripp's dedication, perseverance, and commitment; my gratitude knew no bounds when she welcomed me into the Global Read Aloud community.

If you're one of the readers who asked what happened to the characters from *The Bridge Home*, you'll know I've kept my promise to give one of them a guest appearance in this novel. And whether you're a first-time reader of my work or not, my sincere thanks to you for picking up my book.

Deepest appreciation to those who helped strengthen my research by sharing insights from their experiences teaching in prisons, arranging for feedback from those who have served time, providing comments, or allowing me to glimpse prison life and meet people who were incarcerated: Mr. Ako Mutota and Mrs. Fanta Mutota, Ms. Chandra, Ms. Cheryl Ann Quamina-Baptiste, Ms. Dede Fox, and Ms. Tanvi Suresh. I've had the honor of learning from Dr. Bernard Lafayette about his efforts to share Dr. Martin Luther King Jr.'s nonviolence principles with people who were incarcerated, and hearing Ms. Beth Roan share her experiences teaching in correctional facilities. All this surely fed into my work.

Friends and family took time off their busy schedules to serve as beta readers and specifically to look at my portrayal of Muslim characters, including Dr. Uma Ali and Mr. Hyder Ali, Mr. Datoobhoy and Mrs. Rehana Datoobhoy, Dr. Kasseim Muhammad Jacobs, and Dr. Ulrike Lohmann. I can't express how much that meant to me. Sincere appreciation to Armin Arethna, Phil Bildner, Steven Bickmore, Victoria Coe, Leah Henderson, Saadia Faruqi, Sarah J. Donovan, Laurie Rothenberg, and Elly Swartz.

Thanks to Sara LaFleur for her patience and willingness to always assist. Gratitude to Venessa Carson, Carmela Iaria, Trevor Ingerson, Summer Ogata, and Rachel Wease for their enthusiastic support of my work over the years, to Jennifer Bricking for the cover, to the copyeditors, and to everyone else who worked so hard to bring this book to life.

Last but not least, as COVID-19 continues to restrict our movement, I am happier than ever to spend time with my husband and daughter, whose steadfast encouragement and kindness keep me going. You're always there to assist me in whatever way I need. I wouldn't be the same writer if it weren't for you both.